MURDER AT THE LITTLE INN

A ROSE BLAIR MURDER MYSTERY

JUDY KEIGHTLEY

ISBN-13: (Paperback) –978-0-991987-4-4
Publisher: Judy Keightley

ACKNOWLEDGMENTS

There are so many people to acknowledge who have contributed in one way or another to the writing of this, my fifth Rose Blair mystery. Elaine, Rita, and Margo, my long-suffering editors, I give you my heartfelt thanks for finding those mistakes and pulling me up on my grammar.

A big thank you to all my friends who, over endless cups of coffee, patiently listened to me talk about murder, mayhem, and who helped to brainstorm some tricky scenarios.

Thanks to Lynda for bravely putting herself forward to feature in this novel, and to Joanne at The Little Inn for consenting to the use of her lovely Inn as the venue for murder.

I would also like to acknowledge NaNoWriMo who got me into writing full-length novels and made it possible for me to expand my horizons. You are one great organization!

Any errors and omissions are all mine and to this, I humbly apologize

Last, but certainly not least, a huge thank you to my long-suffering husband, Philip, who has to put up with my ponderous moments and help with my lack of computer skills.

I would like to dedicate this book to my dear friend, Jean Woods, who died suddenly last year (2016) She was a wonderful creative spirit, my dearest soul mate and friend.

ONE

Rose opened one sleepy eye and looked at the bedside clock. It was eight o'clock and Tom was still sound asleep and gently snoring beside her. Puff and Ben, their beloved dogs, were also asleep, and Rose was sorely tempted to close her eyes and join them in their slumbers. It was, after all, very warm and snug under their feather duvet and why shouldn't she sleep in, except that Rose always felt guilty.

Why she felt this way was beyond her as they were both retired and had earned the right to be lazy. It was probably just conditioning like Pavlov's dogs or something like that, but anyway, today Rose had promised her friend Julie that she would go to the fitness class with her. Julie had been trying to get Rose out to the classes for years and finally, after resisting so long, she had succumbed and had now been going out every Monday, Wednesday, and Friday and had actually loved every bit of it.

Tom also had started pole walking, and he too had attended a few of the early risers' fitness classes aimed at getting men out, about, and fit. Bayfield was, in fact, absolutely brilliant for offering every type of fitness programme available.

There were Tai Chi, yoga, aerobics, pole walking, and occasionally Zumba classes all year round and the instructors were all fantastic.

Once again, Rose felt privileged to be living in the wonderful village of Bayfield.

Lying snug for a few more minutes, still reluctant to get up. Rose made a mental list of what her itinerary was for the day. The most exciting part of the day was going to be the Literary Festival, but that wasn't until the evening.

After the fitness class, Rose had arranged to meet up with Carrie and Jen to have coffee at the Charles Street Market and then home for lunch with Tom. Thinking of food made Rose go through a visual exercise in what they had in the fridge to eat. Not an awful lot, she thought, and so a grocery shop would probably have to feature somewhere in her day's agenda.

Rose finally got up and padded into the kitchen to put the kettle on for a cup of tea. They always started the day with a lovely cuppa. Puff and Ben stretched and followed her into the kitchen, where she let them out into the garden. It felt positively balmy outside; maybe Spring was in the air, although Tom always warned her not to be so optimistic. It was not uncommon to have a dump of snow in April, but at least it rarely settled at that time of the year.

She brought the tea into the bedroom, setting it down on Tom's bedside table. He opened his eyes and looked up at Rose and smiled. "Are you going somewhere, love?"

"I'm off to my fitness class and then I'm meeting Carrie and Jen for coffee afterwards. I probably won't be back much before eleven. See you later, love." Rose kissed Tom and left the room.

Cycling to the arena, she found the fitness room positively bulging with people, for many were snowbirds having recently returned from the warmth of Florida, Mexico, or Arizona. The class was as robust as ever. Rose adored the music they played, mostly retro sixties and seventies songs, all from her own era. Sometimes she bopped along to the music, oblivious to the exercise instructions.

By the end of the class, Rose was desperate for a cup of coffee. Saying goodbye to Julie, who couldn't join her for coffee, as she had a doctor's appointment in Goderich, Rose mounted her bicycle and rode to the coffee shop. Jen and Carrie were already inside and waiting for her.

"Hi there you two. When am I going to get you out to fitness class?"

They smiled and shook their heads, "Pole walking is enough for us."

Rose hadn't joined the pole walkers, although she kept meaning to go out with them. Maybe in the summer she would, but then maybe not. The croquet season started the end of May and that would be her main priority.

"So, Carrie and Jen, did you get your tickets for the Literary Festival?" Rose asked while sipping her steaming cup of coffee and munching on a Morning Glory muffin. They really were the best.

"Actually, Mike didn't want to go tonight, and the rest of the weekend is tied up with the family, so, no, we won't be going."

"Neither will I, although I really fancied the Romance Writers Books and Brunch. Never mind, maybe another year." Jen said.

Carrie and Jen both sat on the Town Hall Committee with Rose. She had got to know them quite well since joining the board a couple of years ago. That had been the same year that the murders had taken place when the lead singer of the band called The Berries had been found stabbed to death in what used to be the Town Hall jail. It had been a shocking introduction to the committee but had in a way united the members in adversity. This year they had been incredibly busy during the month of February with the Family Day Soups On followed by the Cabaret. However, March and April had been quiet months, which had enabled the committee to regroup and have more time to prepare for the busy summer ahead.

The women chatted amicably for an hour and then Rose said she had to go. Tom always made fun of the fact that she spent more time talking and having coffee with her friends than actually being at home with him. Rose always retorted that in the summer she had never seen him and had become one of those golf widows. They both laughed about their social lives, saying that they were busier in retirement than they ever had been when working.

Rose cycled home and was greeted by two ecstatic dogs. Tom was just about to take them out for a walk and had them attached to their leashes.

"Don't be too long darling as lunch will be ready shortly," Rose said and disappeared off into the kitchen to make a hasty meal with whatever bits she could find in the fridge. They would be eating out in the evening, so maybe scrambled eggs on toast might be sufficient for lunch, Rose thought, and busied herself with clearing the breakfast things off the table and laying it again for their lunch.

TWO

L ater that day, Rose and Tom walked under a beautiful, clear April evening, unseasonably warm with a star-lit, soft, velvety, inky-black sky. Rose tucked her arm into the crook of Tom's elbow and let out a deep, contented sigh.

"Oh Tom, this evening is absolutely perfect. Just look at the stars; they look like thousands of sparkling diamonds. I'm so looking forward to dinner and meeting the authors. You know, it's been absolutely ages since Bayfield had an author's event. I know that there is the Writer's Festival at the Town Hall, but that's not quite the same as having dinner with the authors!"

Rose had indeed spent the past two dreary winter months counting the days to the Literary Festival being held at Bayfield's historic Little Inn. She loved to read and during the months of November through to April, Rose devoured sometimes as many as three books a week. Thriller and crime novels were her favourite genre and that evening she was to meet two of her very favourite crime writers, Chris Saul and Damian Palmer.

The Blair's turned onto Catherine Street from Bayfield Terrace where they had lived for the past ten years in a house just made with love. Tom and Rose had retired to the village and had fallen head over heels in love with the whole community.

Walking on Catherine Street they came by Lynda and Barry Forbes's house, an unusual con-temporary Frank Lloyd Wright look-a-like built on the corner of Colina Street and Victoria Place. There were no lights on in the house. Rose wondered if they had returned from Florida since Lynda had emailed to say that they were due back in the village that day.

Rose had missed her friend greatly. It had been almost six months since she had last seen her. Texting and emailing had been conducted on a regular basis, but Rose still missed the coffee mornings and shopping trips that they had shared together. In fact, Lynda was Rose's closest friend since the untimely death of Mary.

Rose reflected on how it had been three years since Mary had been so horribly murdered at the Croquet Club. Rose shivered at the ghastly recollection.

Tom looked at her closely and said, "Are you feeling alright, love? You just shivered as if someone had been walking over your grave."

Rose smiled and shrugged her shoulders. "You were close, Tom. I was just thinking about Mary Stokes and her horrible death, so you had part of it right, the grave part I mean..."

They had reached The Little Inn, which, by the number of cars parked outside, was packed. Rose removed her over coat and hung it up on the coat rack down the hallway. Tom kept his leather jacket on and waited for Rose before entering the dining room. The Dinner with Crime Writers was set up in the Willow Room. They were shown to their table. Rose looked around and waved to a few of her friends. Lena and her husband Bob sat at a table across the room. Lena was the Historical Society's archivist and was one of the busiest women in the village. She had helped Rose out with her research on the shipwrecks during the Great Storm of 1913 on more than one occasion and was always so willing to give of her time to the community. Angela, the librarian, sat at the same table as Lena. They were best of friends. Rose waved at them and continued looking around the room. Becky and her husband Jim were sitting with Helen and her husband, Pete. Both women were part of Rose's book club. They had come together shortly after Rose and Tom had moved to the village and now were as much good friends as book club buddies.

Peggy Grierson, the Chair of the Town Hall Committee, was sitting at a table with old Doctor Glover. They made a slightly incongruous pair, Peggy with her stern, old fashioned, and super-efficient manner, and the doctor, old and gnarled, but with still a twinkle in his eyes.

Both had lost their loved ones, and it gladdened Rose's heart greatly to see that both Peggy and the good doctor appeared to be seeing quite a bit of each other. If nothing else, it would assuage the abject loneliness of being left living on your own, Rose thought as she sat down and greeted their fellow guests sitting at the table with them.

They introduced themselves as Sally and Jonathan, Chris Saul's friends. They were a young, hip couple from Toronto and were great followers of Chris and avid readers of all his crime novels.

After the introductions had been made, Rose and Tom settled down. A young waiter, whom Rose recognized as her friend Tanya's grand daughter, came to take their drink orders. Then the evening began, and Rose felt her spirits lift as she absolutely loved reading events, particularly anything to do with crime writers.

After the initial greetings Chris Saul took the podium and started talking about his latest book. Rose felt her attention waning. Chris Saul's voice seemed to drone on and on and, if truth be known, she was actually rather disappointed in him. It wasn't that he was a poor speaker, it was just that he couldn't get one engaged in what he was saying. It was a real shame, as his Inspector Richardson series was great. But the author himself just came across as somewhat arrogant and very full of himself.

Rose caught Tom's eye, and he whispered in her ear, "He's a

pompous twit, but I recognize him from that television show, Money Matters, and he was really good on that."

Almost as if on cue, Chris Saul started to talk about his first career as a financial advisor and how that led to his own television show called Money Matters. As a result of the success of the show, Chris had been able to retire from the finance world and concentrate on his real passion, writing. He had written the first of his Inspector Richardson novels when he was just twenty-six and had never looked back. Now, he was on his tenth book in the series which was set in Winnipeg where Chris himself had grown up.

Sally and Jonathan sitting at Rose and Tom's table, clapped loudly at the conclusion of Chris's speech and Rose noticed that Sally couldn't keep her eyes off the author. According to the short bio on the programme, Chris Saul was married with two young children living in Winnipeg. Rose wondered if he was a serious player with other women, she had her strong suspicions that he most certainly was, if judging by the rapture on their fellow guests' face was anything to go by.

Damian Palmer was the next guest speaker and Rose immediately took to him. He had grown up in England and had the rather self-effacing English manner about him, reminiscent of a young Hugh Grant. Whereas Chris Saul had been openly arrogant and full of himself, Damian Palmer appeared more modest, although he was equally accomplished as Chris Saul. Damian was presently a Professor of Creative Writing at Wilfrid Laurier University. He had made his name riding on the hugely popular wave of vampire writers. His debut novel had been written as a spoof and was called. Suck it and See. It had become an instant hit, and he rapidly churned out another four novels using the same genre. Damian's big break, however, came when he was asked to write a screen play version of Suck it and See.

To his utter amazement, this had proven to be a box office hit, and he hadn't looked back.

. . .

AFTER THE GUEST speakers had finished, Rose and Tom were just getting ready to leave The Little Inn having stayed for the book signing, when they overheard raised voices coming from the bar in the Tap Room. Rose peeped in and saw Damian Palmer and Chris Saul obviously at loggerheads with each other. She couldn't make out what was being said, but both men looked enraged by something.

Doctor Glover and Peggy Grierson were sitting at the bar having a night cap and both looked extremely uncomfortable. Rose caught Peggy's eye and waved to her, mouthing the word 'bye.' Tom fetched Rose's overcoat, and they stepped outside into the cool April night and proceeded to walk home.

"What was all that about?" Tom asked Rose.

"I haven't a clue, but I didn't really like that Chris Saul, I actually found him far too arrogant for my liking," Rose replied as she took Tom's hand and they walked back to their cosy home on Bayfield Terrace.

THREE

The next day was Saturday, and it was The Books and Brunch with Harlequin romance writers, Pippa Hargreaves and Melissa Manson.

Rose disliked the chick-lit romances, but her good friend, Lena, had specifically invited her to go with her to the brunch and Rose hadn't had the heart to decline. Jessica, Rose and Tom's daughter, had bought a ticket for the following day's venue, a children's author's workshop being conducted by none other than the famous writer, Sally Albright the creator of Cyril the Squirrel, the now popular children's television series.

Abby and Ella, Rose and Tom's grandchildren, had the whole collection of Cyril the Squirrel DVD's and Rose had bought both of them stuffed animal characters from the books. Although, the previous Christmas, Abby had been given a Cyril the Squirrel music box, but to Jessica's horror, she had declared that she no longer liked the squirrel and had really wanted a Barbie doll instead. Rose smiled to herself as she remembered her contrary granddaughter denouncing Cyril the Squirrel saying, "Cyril was only for babies!"

The Books and Brunch was being held in the Carriage Room of

The Little Inn and it started at 10:30 a.m. Rose left Tom in bed reading the newspaper with Puff and Ben, their beloved dogs, curled up on the feather duvet beside him.

She had made him some coffee, toasted a bagel, and brought this to him on a tray. Kissing Tom goodbye, Rose quietly left the house and walked down Bayfield Terrace towards Catherine Street.

Passing her friend Lynda Forbes' house, she saw lights on in the kitchen. Oh, good, Rose thought, they're back. She would pop in to see her friend after the brunch.

Once again, The Little Inn was packed with people, although this time, there were no men in sight. Rose spotted Lena right away. Her friend always looked slightly eccentric with a penchant for brightly coloured scarves which she always wore tied bandana style around her hair. She also loved to wear totally over the top jewellery.

Today was no exception. Lena sported a black and white head band and a turquoise blue jacket. Around her neck she wore a purple and white chunky necklace and in her ears she had long, dangly, and lilac coloured feather earrings. She looked like a breath of fresh air, and Rose loved her for all her eccentricity and creativity.

Lena had managed to grab a spot right up next to the head table where the two authors sat, looking suitably nervous and uncomfortable. Rose picked up the programme and read their names, Pippa Hargreaves and Sally Manson.

Pippa took to the floor first and introduced herself. She was a very attractive thirty-something with a mane of shoulder length, glossy, thick chestnut hair which framed her small face. She had the biggest eyes that Rose had ever seen, a pert nose and pink rose bud lips, which gave her a doll like appearance.

Pippa had written her first Harlequin Romance ten years ago and had called it, The Sins of Sexy Suzy. She claimed that the story was based on a friend that she used to know when she was a nurse at Clinton Hospital and her name was Suzy. The book had been an instant success and had inspired Pippa to write a further twenty novels all in the same red-hot genre. It seemed to Rose that there was a definite recipe to follow when writing romances, and once you had read one, they all appeared similar. Maybe she should try writing a novel, and then she smiled at the thought of Tom's reaction to reading it. No, she definitely would not become an author of steamy novels or, for that matter, any others.

Melissa Manson stood up and started her talk. Just like Chris Saul the previous evening, Melissa seemed unable to engage the audience sufficiently and Rose soon found herself distracted by something going on in the lobby of The Little Inn. Making her excuses to Lena, Rose got up and quietly left the room. In the lobby, a young girl, obviously one of the staff members, was sitting on a chair in open distress. She had been crying and clutched a great wad of Kleenex tissues. Another staff member was busy talking to someone on the phone and by the look on her face, she too was in distress.

"What is the matter?" Rose said quietly, while kneeling beside her.

"I've just found one of our guests dead in his room. He was just lying there with his eyes wide open. I knew that he was dead the minute I walked into the room." She started to choke up again, so Rose patted her shoulder and gave her another Kleenex.

"It's always a shock seeing someone dead." Rose said, remembering the previous summer when she herself had found her friend, Laura Du Preez, floating by the side of their boat in the marina with a shot gun wound.

"Who was he?" she asked the young girl.

"Well, um.... I'm not sure that I should be telling you, but the dead man was one of the authors from last night's reading. Chris Saul is his name. Theresa is just calling the police and they will have to deal with all the formalities."

The manager of The Little Inn walked in, and Rose decided that it was time for her to go. She slipped back to the table and whispered in Lena's ear that she had to leave.

Walking back home, Rose couldn't help thinking about Chris Saul and how he was now dead. She wondered quite how he had died. It seemed almost unbelievable that he was dead, particularly as he had appeared just fine the night before. Hopefully her good friend DCI Susan Parker might be able to elaborate more on the cause of his death.

He lay peaceful in death; white on white, almost like a staged piece of modelling for an artist's painting. The white cotton sheet was bunched up in his hands, which seemed to clasp his chest almost as if in prayer. He could have been asleep if it hadn't had been for those glassy eyes just staring into infinity, and his mouth slightly open as if to receive his last breath.

One bare leg hung carelessly over the side of the queen-sized bed, the other stretched to full length. His clothes, shirt, underpants, and trousers lay in a crumpled heap in the middle of the room His shoes, tossed off his feet, lay separately, one by the door, the other at the base of the bed. Two wine glasses sat on the pine bedside table nesting up to the lamp which had been left on.

Chris Saul had died the same way as he had been born, stark naked, but the big difference was that in birth he had taken his first breath quite naturally, in death, his last breath had been forced out of him in a quite unnatural way.

FOUR

When Rose returned home, Tom was nowhere to be seen, neither were the dogs. It didn't take too much deductive reasoning to know that he had taken them for a walk. Rose looked around the kitchen and sighed, thinking that it was time to redecorate the room. It was beginning to look tired, much like me, Rose thought, as she pulled out the ingredients to make a spaghetti pie for their dinner the next day when Jessica would be over with Abby and Ella, their granddaughters. She would make the pie and then a large chocolate and walnut cake.

While Rose chopped onions and peppers, she couldn't help thinking about Chris Saul and wondering why he had died. She was absolutely itching to ask her friend Susan, but it would be too soon for even the police to know the cause of death. There was always a set procedure involved after the discovery of any dead body.

Rose had witnessed this too many times over the years and knew that autopsies and forensic reports, not to mention the coroner's report, all had to be written up before the police would announce the cause of death. Even then, the next of kin had to be notified before it became public knowledge.

Still, Rose thought, I will call Susan later today and maybe invite her around for drinks. That way she could gently prod her for details.

Detective Chief Inspector Susan Parker had been lounging around her living room in her red satin pyjamas, listening to music.

Today it was Leslie Feist, her current favourite female singer. She had known Leslie briefly when she had lived in Roncesvalles, Toronto. Well, not really known her, but she had frequented the same pub and Susan had been quite impressed when she had found out that Leslie was a well-known singer.

She picked up The Globe and Mail and started to read the travel section. It was Saturday, and she had the whole glorious weekend stretching out ahead of her. Susan was going to meet up with her boyfriend, Peter, and they planned to eat dinner at the Japanese restaurant, Drift, and then take in a show at The Park Theatre in Goderich. The phone rang, and it was, therefore, with great reluctance that she answered it and saw on the screen that it was indeed the Serious Crimes division, her department in London, contacting her.

"Detective Parker speaking," Susan answered crisply as she drummed her fingers on the telephone table. For crying out loud, she thought, it was her weekend off, was there never any rest for the wicked? After receiving instructions from the despatcher, she dashed upstairs and quickly got dressed. A man had been found dead in his bedroom at The Little Inn and foul play was suspected.

Susan lived across the Bayfield River in one of the Harbour Court condos. She had moved to the village of Bayfield from London after the tragic death of her fiancé, Henri Le Bruin, a fellow police officer of the Montreal Sûreté. Before that, she had been the proud owner of a pretty Ontario cottage on Edward Street in Wortley Village, London.

Her whole world had been turned upside down with the death of Henri. She had retired from the police force but had been asked to come back out of retirement when the body of a South African woman had been found in the Bayfield Marina. That had been a complicated case and had involved CSIS.

Susan had, in fact, been very attracted to Andrew Ryan, a married man, head of the CSIS unit assigned to the Bayfield case. He was based in Ottawa and lived there with his wife and children. She had met up with him just once after the wrap up of the Bayfield investigation. That had been when Susan and he had both been attending a conference on Homeland Security in Toronto. Although the chemistry was fantastic between them, by mutual consent, they had both decided to not continue a long-distance relationship and in a way Susan had been relieved. She had been down that road before and it had not ended well.

She drove past the docks and onto the highway, turning right onto Short Hill and then onto Bayfield Terrace. Driving past her friends Tom and Rose Blair's house, Susan fleetingly wondered how they were both getting on. She had been so busy at work since her promotion to Detective Chief Inspector. Having been sent on endless conferences and workshops, she barely had time to think, let alone socialize. Indeed, her personal relationship with Peter Joyce had also suffered, but at least he understood the nature of the beast being himself on call twenty-four hours a day as a police photographer.

Susan pulled up outside The Little Inn. Of all the historic buildings in Bayfield, The Little Inn stood out as her absolute favourite. Built in 1832 as a stagecoach inn, the place positively oozed gracious charm and tranquility. It looked like a dwelling that one would find in the Deep South, somewhere like Atlanta or Georgia. Thoughts of Gone with the Wind always flickered into Susan's mind when passing The Little Inn.

She entered the building and immediately noticed that there was an event going on in the Willow Room. There were loads of women sitting at tables eating breakfast. Stacks of books were piled on a table in the middle of the room and two attractive thirty somethings were busy signing the books.

The manager of The Little Inn tapped Susan on her shoulder and beckoned her to follow her upstairs. To Susan's surprise there was yellow tape draped across the doorway to room number 3 and a man wearing protective clothing, complete with white paper booties and disposable gloves was hovering over a body which lay supine on the bed. How could the pathologist have got here so quickly from London? Susan thought as she ducked under the tape and entered the room.

The stranger turned and held out his hand. "Hi, I'm Ian, Dr. Green, just covering for your usual pathologist. I live in Goderich, which is why I got the call and was able to get here so quickly."

"Well, I'm DCI Parker. I was wondering how you got here so quickly as I live in the village myself."

Susan approached the body and bent over to take a closer look. "So, who have we here?"

Ian read from his notes. "Apparently this is a Chris Saul from Winnipeg. He was here for the Literary Festival. In fact, I believe that he was one of the guest speakers last night, ironically a crime writer."

That takes the biscuit, Susan thought as she pulled on her latex gloves and gently pulled back the sheet.

"Have you any thoughts yet on the time of death, um... Ian, Doctor Green?" Susan had noticed a thermometer in his hand.

"I would say by his body temperature, plus the fact that rigor mortis has set in, that the time of death would have been at least eight to ten hours ago, maybe somewhere between twelve and two in the morning."

"And what are the causes of his death?"

The doctor paused before answering. "For all intents and purposes, every indication points to a heart attack, yet I don't know..."

"What is it you don't know?" Susan said impatiently. The good doctor was beginning to irritate her as he was just being so pedantic.

"Well, for a start, he's a young man, a fit one at that. I can't put my finger on it, but his death doesn't sit well with me. The autopsy results will tell me exactly what he died of and the circumstances of his death, but right now, don't rule out foul play."

Susan nodded and then looked around the room. Seeing two wine glasses sitting on the bedside table, she thought to herself, this man probably had sex just before he died, and then she thought, well that's not a bad way to exit the world. Her thoughts were interrupted by the arrival of the police photographer, none other than her boyfriend, Peter Joyce.

Susan smiled at him and said, "He's all yours," and then she turned to speak to the police officer who had just arrived.

"Oh ... Sergeant, did you bring the evidence bags? We will need to collect a few things here for DNA sampling."

"Is it a case of murder, ma'am? Has the SOC team been called out?" he asked.

"We're not sure, but Dr. Green here is certainly going to explore all possibilities. I'll leave you now to do your work while I go to speak to the management."

Susan caught Peter's eye. As she made her way to the door, he winked at her and smiled that lopsided smile of his that always got her heart racing.

"Nice meeting you, Dr. Green. Please send me the autopsy results as soon as possible." Susan said and with that DCI Parker left the room and headed for the stairs. Back in the lobby area, Susan poked her head into the dining room where large numbers of women were still gathered.

She beckoned to a waiter, who was carrying a tray of coffee into the room. "What's going on? Why are all these women here?"

The waiter pointed to a large poster board sitting on an easel just inside the dining room. A rather garish purple and gold printed billboard read "Bayfield Literary Festival" followed by the names of the guest speakers. Susan immediately saw Chris Saul's name on the list.

The waiter, as if reading her mind, said, "Yes, the dead man, that's him, the crime writer, Chris Saul." He said this with a rather disdainful voice.

"You sound as if you didn't like the man?" Susan said as she picked up one of the programmes sitting on the side table.

"Oh, well, I don't like to talk ill of the dead, but he was very rude to the staff, just strutted around as if he owned the place."

"Were you on duty last night?"

"Yes, and before you ask, the evening went well until the end, when our dead man got all bolshie with the other writer, Damian Palmer. They almost came to blows with each other. If you ask me, that Chris was a nasty piece of work."

Susan thanked him and said that an officer would take a full statement later, but in the meantime, she would like a complete list of everyone attending the Crime Writer's dinner. Just as she was giving the waiter instructions, the owner of The Little Inn appeared carrying a sheet of paper. She was a beautiful woman with an ethereal air of calm about her. Her pale blonde hair was tied back in a ponytail, and she wore little make up. Susan couldn't help but wonder how someone so young could be the owner of such a prestigious inn.

"Here you are," she said, "I'm Joanne. If I can be of any assistance, please contact me anytime." With that, she pressed her business card into Susan's hand.

So cool and calm in the face of death, Susan thought as she looked at the sheet of paper Joanne had given to her. It was, indeed, a list of all the guests booked into the Inn as well as a complete list of people attending the Literary Festival for the whole weekend.

Susan prepared to leave, but just as she was stepping outside, she bumped into the SOC team carrying all their paraphernalia. Soon the lovely peaceful inn would well and truly become a crime scene. It was time to get her own team together, Susan thought, and to secure an incident room. The Lion's Club had always been very accommodating. Their meeting room was perfect. Susan crossed her fingers as she punched in The Lion's Club's president's number. At this stage, she didn't even know for sure if it was a murder they were investigating, but something told her that Chris Saul's death was by no means natural.

FIVE

Rose had just taken the chocolate cake out of the oven when the telephone rang. The minute that she put the phone to her ear, she just knew that it was her sister Kate from Kelowna, B.C. Kate had a very distinctively loud voice although, this time, it sounded strained and decidedly quivery.

"What's wrong, Kate?" Rose asked, suddenly feeling rather panicky. Her sister was usually so upbeat and cheerful.

"Rose.... Oh, Rose," she sobbed. "Bob's left me. He's gone off with my friend, Natalie." Kate began to emit huge heart rendering sobs down the phone.

Rose couldn't believe that Bob, gentle Bob who farmed Alpacas and grew vegetables, the man who couldn't kill their chickens as they had all become family pets, could do this. How could she reconcile that same Bob with a wife cheating, friend stealing adulterer?

"Oh, Kate, my darling, what are you going to do? Maybe it's just a male menopausal thing and he'll come to his senses and realize what a fool he's been."

"I said all of that to him and he just turned around and said that he loved Natalie and he hadn't loved me for a long time." Kate began to cry again. "Oh, Rose, he was so cold to me. He felt like a stranger."

"Now, Kate, you need to get away and come over here for a while. Maybe putting some distance between you will give Bob the time to come to his senses and cool off. Please come."

There was silence on the other end of the line and then a loud sniff before Kate finally spoke. "Are you really sure that you wouldn't mind putting me up for a couple of weeks? I would truly love to get away from all of this."

"Yes, of course, you must come and soon. You can see Ally when you're here."

Rose put the phone down and went back into the kitchen. She actually felt quite shaken. Bob and Kate had seemed so happy last time Rose and Tom had seen them. Their children will be absolutely devastated, Rose thought, particularly young Ally who was at Western University in London. Oh dear, oh dear, Rose thought, her poor sister Kate.

She just got back to preparing dinner when the phone rang again. This time it was her friend, Lynda Forbes.

"Hi, Rose, I'm back."

"Yes, I saw your lights on this morning and meant to drop by, but I got side-tracked. Oh, Lynda, I've so missed you. Did you have a great time in West Palm Beach?"

"Yes, we did, but we also went to Panama for a couple of weeks, and I really loved it. Look, would you and Tom like to come around for drinks tonight, say around eight o'clock."

Rose glanced at her planner. The evening was indeed free. Jessica and the children would be arriving the following morning, but drinks with Lynda and Barry would definitely be doable.

Tom returned with the dogs, and Rose told him all about Kate and Bob. Tom really liked Bob, and he was as shocked as Rose. It all seemed so out of character.

"Oh, Tom, he actually told Kate that he hadn't loved her for years. Wasn't that a cruel thing to say?"

Tom just shook his head.

"Oh, and Tom, I almost forgot, that author, what's his name, ummm... oh, yes, you know the one we thought was arrogant?"

"Chris Saul, do you mean?" Tom said.

"Yes, well, he was found dead in his bedroom this morning. I was there when they found him."

"I wondered what all those police cars were doing parked outside The Little Inn. Susan Parker's car was also there when I walked past a short time ago. Well, I hope that it's not another murder in Bayfield."

Tom had bad memories of the spate of murders that had happened in the village over the last five years.

First, there had been the scuba diver found dead on the beach down from Pioneer Park. It was Ben, their dog, who had dug the body up and it was Tom himself who had found the decomposing copse.

Then there was the awful case of Rose's friend, Mary Stokes, who had been killed by a crossbow shot into her chest when she was at the Croquet Club. That had been a bizarre case involving Interpol and Serbian terrorists.

The following year, the well-known lead singer of the group, The Berries, was murdered at the Town Hall and the fitness instructor, Gillian Jeffries, was also found dead. With thoughts of the fitness instructor, Tom had mixed feelings. Gillian Jeffries had come on to him strongly while Rose was away in Halifax. He now squirmed at the memory and at how close he had been to betraying his vows.

The last tragic murder had been the double deaths of Rose and Tom's good friends from southwest Africa, the Du Preez's. It was Rose who had been shaken up badly by the discovery of Laura Du Preez floating in the water by the side of their boat in the marina.

He had, himself, found Andre Du Preez shot to death in his car parked on Pavilion Road and that had knocked the stuffing out of him, too.

After that gruesome summer, Rose and Tom had sworn never to get involved ever again with any crime related incidences in the village.

SIX

Susan looked around the room at her team. It had been nothing short of a miracle getting everyone together in a space of four hours, much of which had been spent on the phone. It was just amazing what could be achieved by proxy, Susan thought as she stood up, preparing to speak to her fellow officers.

There had been a few changes to the team from the previous year. Sergeant Mathieson had been transferred to the Serious Crimes Unit in Milton with no love lost on Susan's part. She had heard through the grapevine that he had applied for a position with CSIS but had been turned down.

Constable's Brown and Elliot, who seconded to her from the OPP, sat smiling and looking bright eyed and bushy tailed. Next to them, a new member sat apprehensively, nervous, and looking highly uncomfortable. Constable Holly Ryan was relatively new to the police force, having only joined up the previous year. She was only twenty four but had already proven herself by coming in top of the class at the academy, beating all the male graduates by far. Her speciality, however, was in IT. She wanted to become a communication specialist.

Sergeant Flowers was indeed the only senior officer available to join the team. He had always previously worked with Sergeant Mathieson and had rather been in his shadow. Maybe now he might be able to shine by himself, Susan thought as she cleared her throat, ready to speak.

"Good afternoon, everyone. I think that you all know each other, apart from our new team member, DC Holly Ryan, who comes to us from the London Serious Crimes unit. Welcome Holly. We'll just go around the table and introduce ourselves."

Introductions done, Susan continued her speech, "You all know that the body of Chris Saul, a crime writer, was found in his bedroom at The Little Inn last night. Doctor Green, the medical pathologist from Goderich, is running tests to see if he can find the cause of death. Outwardly, it looks as if he died of a heart attack, but Doctor Green has suspicions of foul play. He promised to email any preliminary results to us just as soon as they come in."

"As usual, with any murder enquiry, and in this case, potential murder enquiry, expediency is the word. All the guests present at The Little Inn Crime Writer's dinner need to be interviewed, as do all the staff. Constables Brown and Elliot, I give you this task."

"Constable Ryan, I want you to research Chris Saul's background thoroughly and check his cell phone and computer. I want to know everything about the man, both in his private and public life.

"Sergeant Flowers, I would like you to interview all the guest speakers at the Literary Festival. See if you can find any connection to the deceased. Okay, go to it everyone and be back here by eight o'clock tomorrow morning."

After the team had departed, Susan was left alone with her thoughts. She opened up her laptop to check for emails. Sure enough there was an email from Dr. Green telling her that he had the results of the blood work back and that there were definite traces of potassium chloride and strong traces of Flunitrazepam, commonly known as Rohypnol or 'roofies', the date–rape drug, in his system. Potassium chloride would account for the outward signs of heart failure. The Flunitrazepam would have been used as a sedative or a strong sleeping pill.

He had also found a tiny puncture mark under the chin of the deceased, consistent with a syringe insertion. This was most certainly a case of murder by lethal injection.

SEVEN

Lynda and Barry Forbes greeted Rose and Tom effusively. They both looked tanned and relaxed. Lynda wore a casual colourful wrap-around skirt in shades of emerald green shot through with yellow. She looked like an exotic bird. Even though it was still April, Barry wore bright blue, flowery Bermuda shorts. Rose looked at Tom and herself attired in winter clothes and realized just how drab and dowdy they looked in comparison.

Drinks were poured out, and the men started to talk about golf, leaving Rose and her friend Lynda to catch up.

"Did you go to the Literary Festival?" Lynda asked Rose. She knew that Rose just loved to read and how excited she had been when they had first heard about the festival being held at the Little Inn.

"Yes, I went to two of the workshops. Oh, and Jessica is coming over tomorrow to attend the children's writer's workshop. But it was rather awful. Lynda, one of the authors died, apparently sometime Friday night. His name was Chris Saul. He wrote the Inspector Richardson series which I really liked."

Lynda looked really shocked. "Rose, did you say his name was

Chris Saul? I used to know someone of that name many years ago. If I remember rightly, he was a real jerk. Mind you, that was over ten years ago, and he was quite young then. I never knew that he was a crime writer though. Maybe it's not the same Chris Saul. Fancy that."

"Oh, he talked about being in finance before his writing days. He was really quite full of himself. Tom remembers him being on a television show called Money Matters. He says that he was quite good."

"That's quite shocking news, Rose. Do they know how he died? He couldn't have been more than about thirty-five. Was it a drug overdose or too much alcohol, maybe? I do remember that he drank like a fish."

"How did you actually know him, Lynda?" Rose asked.

"We worked in the same office, DFI, Financial Advisors, on York Street in Toronto."

"I can't exactly see you working in finance. I thought that you were into interior designing?"

"Oh, dear Rose, I've worked in so many places. I even worked for the Yellow Pages at one stage!" Lynda laughed and poured Rose out another glass of wine.

"Fancy that," Rose said as she nibbled at one of the delicious canapés sitting on a beautiful pottery plate on the low-level coffee table in their living room. It was of Aztec design, with llamas and snakes entwined around the base and golden eagles souring in the background.

Lynda saw Rose admiring her pottery.

"Rose, I have a small gift for you." And she handed Rose a circular object wrapped up in tissue paper. Inside was a smaller version of the same Aztec bowl that Rose had just been admiring.

"I know that you love pottery, and I just couldn't resist this. We bought quite a lot of trinkets and things from Panama."

"Oh, it's beautiful. Thank you so much. Now tell me all about your holiday in Panama and your stay in West Palm Beach. I just know that I'm going to feel green with envy, you lucky thing escaping our yucky winter."

They had indeed had a long and extremely cold winter with loads of snow and more than enough blizzards to last a lifetime. Twice the highway had been closed both north and south of the village. The actual winter conditions didn't bother Rose and Tom so much as the length of time that the winters spanned. Starting the previous November with the first dump of snow through to the end of March, five months of snowy weather and, technically, winter still wasn't yet over. Oh, to be a snowbird, Rose thought, although Tom and she had talked about maybe heading south for three months, it was always the dogs that prevented them from going, that and the lousy exchange rate. Quite a few of their friends who had always gone to Florida in the past now had stopped going, as it was just too expensive. Rose sighed as she listened to Lynda talk about their trip to Panama. Now that was one place that she would dearly love to visit one day, she thought as she scoffed down another wonderful canapé.

The evening ended and Rose and Tom thanked Lynda and Barry for everything. Rose suggested that they meet up for coffee later that week and Lynda said that she would have to see when her bridge games were scheduled. The men shook hands and Rose gave Lynda a big hug.

"It's great to have you back in town. I really missed you."

Tom and Rose Blair walked to Bayfield Terrace and back to their cosy house content with the pleasant evening spent with their friends, the Forbes.

EIGHT

DCI Susan Parker had spent her evening and night with Peter Joyce. First, they went out to eat at the small Japanese restaurant in the village called Drift. It had opened the previous summer and had soon become a popular eating place with the locals. After their meal they had driven over to Goderich and watched the latest James Bond movie showing at The Park Theatre in the Square. Returning to her condo, Susan poured out a night cap for both of them and they flopped down on the comfy sofa and began to chat.

"Did you take enough photographs of that man at The Little Inn, Peter? By the way, it does look like murder. The pathologist has found traces of potassium chloride in his blood."

"Who was he?" Peter asked.

"His name is Chris Saul. He was an author attending the Literary Festival being held at The Little Inn."

"Chris Saul, that name sounds familiar. Didn't he host a show called Money Matters?

"Money Matters? I didn't know that. I thought that his only pause for fame was writing crime novels?"

"Oh well, the poor man's dead now, but there is something about him that's niggling at the back of my mind. I'm sure that it's something to do with finances. It will come to me. Right now, though, I'm in the mood for love..."

"Simply because you're near me," Susan sang out as she cuddled up to Peter and gave him a kiss.

"Let's go to bed," Peter said huskily as he took Susan's hand and began walking towards the stairs.

It crossed Susan's mind that they were both behaving like a married couple. Gone was that primal urgency and passion of six months ago when they would have made love there on the sofa with complete and utter abandonment. She couldn't stop herself from thinking that maybe Peter Joyce was becoming just a tad boring.

The next morning, Rose and Tom woke to birds singing and a beautiful blue sky. They had slept in, and it was already nine o'clock when Rose made a cup of tea for both of them. Jessica and the girls would be arriving soon.

The Children's Author workshop started at 10:30 a.m. and went on to around 1:00 p.m.

Tom and Rose had just finished eating their breakfast when the front door burst open causing Ben and Puff to bark loudly as Abby and Ella came rushing in like two little dervishes.

"Grandma, Grandpa, we're going to see Cyril the Squirrel," Ella shouted. Jessica and Abby followed Ella into the kitchen.

"Oh, hi Mom and Dad. Ella is convinced that she's going to see Cyril the Squirrel. Abby says she doesn't want to see the yucky squirrel, but I can't get them to understand that neither of them will be seeing any squirrels and that it's just me going to a workshop."

Rose and Tom smiled. What would little girls of six and eight know about workshops?

"Now Abby and Ella, you're going to stay with Grandma and Grandpa, and we can take Puff and Ben for a walk together. I'm sure that mummy will bring you back the latest Cyril the Squirrel book for you to read."

Ella stamped her little foot and shouted, "I want to see Cyril."

Abby retorted, "Cyril is just for babies."

"He's not," Ella screamed and ran out of the kitchen into the sunroom where Puff and Ben had retreated and were currently curled up like bookends on the sofa.

Rose whispered to Jessica, "Just go, darling, they'll be fine. Creep out before Ella sees you leave."

Jessica took her mothers advice and quietly closed the front door behind her as she headed for her car.

"Right, who wants a game of Dominoes?" Tom said as he cleared the breakfast plates off the table and prepared to play Dominoes.

"Oh Grandpa, I'll play with you." Abby said demurely. Rose left the two playing while she went into the sunroom to talk to Ella.

"So, Ella, what do you fancy doing? What about some colouring in? I bought some new crayons and markers especially for you."

Ella was silent for a minute and then she smiled a big, wide smile which showed her gappy teeth.

"I'm going to draw a picture of Cyril the Squirrel and then we can go and give it to him, can't we Grandma?"

Rose laughed. Her grand daughter was as stubborn as a mule. She never gave up on anything!

"Okay, missy. Go and create a masterpiece for that squirrel."

With that Ella set to work with a determined expression on her face.

Meanwhile, at The Little Inn, Jessica was enjoying her time out from being a busy mother. She rarely managed to escape from the children at weekends, although since Ella had started school, Jessica had at least managed to work some day shifts at the hospital. She was a qualified nurse and had been only able to work the odd weekend when Rob could look after the girls until both were at school. So, today's workshop was a rare treat; three blissful hours with no demands from either her husband or the girls.

Sally Albright, author of the very popular Cyril the Squirrel, series, was all business. Jessica couldn't help but notice that she was dressed like a CEO of some large corporation. Sally wore a taupe-coloured suit with the jacket buttoned up high on her neck with a matching pencil slim knee-length skirt. High, glossy black stilettos adorned her feet. Her dark brown hair was worn back in a tight chignon and her talon like fingernails were painted a bright, blood red.

According to her bio on the programme, Sally Albright had been born in England in 1981. She had immigrated to Canada in 2007, and the following year, at the age of twenty-seven, had published her first Cyril the Squirrel book. This had become an immediate hit and within three years Sally had not only written a further five books, but Cyril the Squirrel had been turned into a very popular television show.

All the merchandizing imaginable had followed with every type of soft toy made in the likeness of Cyril, plus t-shirts and hats all bearing the squirrel logo.

It was positively mind boggling what a frenzy the whole Cyril the Squirrel thing had created, but Sally Albright, thought Jessica, looked like she'd sucked a sour lemon. Her mouth sagged downwards, and her dark brown eyes flashed with impatience. Despite the huge success of her creation, Sally Albright did not appear to be a happy woman.

The brunch served at The Little Inn was positively delicious. Fresh fruit compote, warm quiche, stuffed crepes with cranberries and goats' cheese, Greek and Caesar salads, and then to follow, lemon tart, strawberry Pavlova, and chocolate mousse cake.

Sally's talk was interesting. Even though Jessica could not warm to the author, her talent was obvious and her rise to fame reflected her sheer tenacity and business acumen. Like most success stories, Sally had worked jolly hard to make it all happen. She also knew that Cyril's popularity was waning so that her latest creation, yet to be published, was a Mouse called Molly. Jessica just knew that Ella would fall head over heals in love with Molly the Mouse the minute that Sally had shown the illustrations to the captivated audience. Molly was such a girlie looking mouse with long, curly eyelashes and rosebud lips. She was dressed in a pink gingham pinafore dress slightly reminiscent of a Beatrix Potter creation.

"Molly is like the daughter that I never had," Sally Albright said, and for one minute her hard veneer cracked as she wistfully continued, "I was married very briefly, not long enough to have a child of my own, so Molly is my substitute."

Jessica could already see the cute Molly the Mouse cuddly toys and all the rest of the merchandize and branding that went along with any new venture. Move over Cyril, Molly is coming, she thought while lining up with over thirty other women all waiting to buy one of Sally's latest books and have her autograph them. She had just reached the head of the line when Ella came running into the room holding a picture in her hand.

"Mummy, Mummy, I've done a picture for Cyril the Squirrel. Where is he? Can I give it to him?"

Sally Albright looked up from signing her autograph and shrieked at the top of her voice, "Get this effing child out of here this minute!"

Jessica was so shocked by the horrible tone of her voice that she just froze. Ella stood there not sure what had just happened, when Rose came rushing in. She was greeted by what looked like a staged tableau. Dozens of women all looking at Sally Albright absolutely aghast at what they had just heard.

"Oh, there you are Ella. You shouldn't have just run in here by yourself darling. Um... Jessica, I'll take her back home. She just wanted to give this picture to Cyril the Squirrel, that's all."

Rose caught Ella's hand and proceeded to pull her towards the door. Jessica grabbed her purse and ran out following her mother.

Tom stood outside The Little Inn with Puff, Ben, and Abby waiting patiently for Ella and Rose to return.

"Just what was all that about?" Rose asked Jessica when they were out of ear shot of the dining room.

"Oh, mom, that Sally Albright was just horrid. She shouted at Ella using totally inappropriate language. Considering that she is a world-renowned children's author she needs to control her anger."

Rose looked at Ella who seemed unfazed by the turn of events.

"Are you alright, darling?" She said while putting her hand in Ella's and gently walking her down Catherine Street away from the Inn and towards Bayfield Terrace and their home.

"I'm starving, grandma." Ella said and started to skip along the side of the road. "Do we have 'pagetti pie for dinner?"

She had asked the management if she could delay checking out of The Little Inn until at least mid-afternoon. The Children's Author workshop had finished at one which would give her time to have a rest before hitting the road and driving back to Toronto.

The workshop had gone as planned until that little brat of a girl had run in and spoilt the whole book signing, Sally thought as she lay on her bed in her room nursing one almighty headache. She suddenly felt just so incredibly sleepy. She had just had that one glass of wine at the bar just before coming up to her room and now she could barely keep her eyes open...

NINE

DCI Susan Parker looked around the room at her team assembled before her. It had now been just over twenty-four hours since the murder of Chris Saul, the crime writer, and time was ticking by far too quickly. The general rule of thumb in the Police Force was if you couldn't make headway in the first couple of days of an enquiry then you may never be able to solve the crime.

"Right, everyone, let's have your reports. Constables Elliot and Brown, what did you learn from the guests staying at The Little Inn last Friday?

Constable Elliot stood up and opened his notebook. He cleared his throat once and then began reading from his notes, "We managed to interview everyone who had attended the Crime Writers Dinner, all fifty of them. There was nothing significant other than the fact that all the people interviewed were big fans of one or other of the authors.

A Doctor Glover and a Peggy Grierson were having a night cap at the bar when the deceased started shouting at Damian Palmer. He apparently accused him of plagiarism and said that he was going to expose him to the public.

"Damian Palmer told him to go to hell and then Chris went to hit Damian and the waiter had to quickly intervene. The Doctor and his friend were both quite shocked by the man's behaviour. They said that he appeared irrational and maybe had been drinking too much. Another guest," Constable Elliot looked down at his notes again, "a Rose Blair, also stated that she had heard raised voices coming from the bar area. She reckoned that the two men were having a fight over something. That's all I have to report, Ma'am."

Constable Brown stood up and added, "I interviewed the barman and the waiter, Ma'am, and both men said that Chris Saul had been drinking heavily and that he was definitely trying to provoke a fight with Damian Palmer. They said that Chris' behaviour was rude and aggressive. He was the one that had started the fight and was champing for more. After they had stopped the fight, Damian had left the room and Chris ordered another drink before looking at his watch and then going upstairs presumably to his bedroom. That was the last they saw of him. That's all I have, Ma'am."

The two Constables sat down. Susan stood up, "Thank you, now what about Constable Ryan, what have you to share with us?"

Constable Ryan looked even more nervous today than yesterday, Susan thought as she waited for her to report to the team.

She stood up and coughed to clear her throat before beginning to read directly from her laptop. "Chris Saul was born in Winnipeg in 1980, making him 37 years old. He had a normal childhood, his father worked in a bank, the RBC, and his mother was a Kindergarten teacher. He had one brother, younger by two years. Chris went to the University of Windsor and studied maths and economics. He graduated in 2002 and then got a job as a Financial Advisor for DFI in Windsor. He climbed the ladder quite rapidly and by the age of 24 he had been made Senior Advisor. He wrote his first novel, Money Matters at the age of 25, and was asked to head up a television show of the same name. He continued working for DFI but was transferred to the Toronto office in 2005. In 2008 he left the financial world to concentrate on his writing. His Inspector Richardson series had taken off in popularity."

Constable Ryan paused a moment to take a breath and then continued to read from her computer. "He married Sally Albright," there was a stunned silence as the team took in this information, "but they were only married for one year. He remarried again in 2012 to Jane White of Winnipeg and they now have two small children, Hannah, aged four and Neil, aged two. Chris Saul has written ten Inspector Richardson novels and two Money Matters books. That's all I've got for now, Ma'am."

Constable Ryan's cheeks were flushed a deep red and her eyes sparkled. It had taken much effort on her part to disseminate her notes to the team, but she had succeeded and now felt infused with success.

DCI Parker stood up and thanked Constable Ryan. Looking at her notes she then called upon Sergeant Flowers to report on his interviews with the guest speakers of the Literary Festival. He stood up and produced a sheet of typed paper. Pulling out a pair of reading glasses he proceeded to read from his notes.

"There were five guest speakers booked for the festival. Two each for the Dinner with the Author, on Friday night, and two for the romance writers with the Books and Brunch, on Saturday morning. Only one author was booked for the children's writer's workshop on the Sunday. When I interviewed Damian Palmer, he was still in a state of shock over the death of Chris Saul. He openly admitted to not liking the man, but he respected his work none the less. He had been asleep in his room on the other side of The Little Inn guest suites at the time of the deceased death. Of course, because it was in the middle of the night, there was no one around to give him an alibi, but he did appear genuinely shocked and unless he is a really good actor, I believed him."

DCI Parker interrupted Sergeant Flowers, "Did you ask him about the fight in the bar?"

Sergeant Flowers nodded and continued to read from his notes. "Yes, I asked him what the argument was about, and he told me that Chris Saul had accused him of plagiarism. According to Chris, Damian's latest book made references to a small town in Ontario called Alliston, and a farmhouse there which Chris had written about in his Inspector Richardson series. Damian said that it was laughable really to be accused of plagiarism as he had written from his first-hand experience of staying at the farm with his wife. The farmhouse had been converted into a bed, breakfast, and spa and offered couple's retreats. Another interesting piece of information Damian imparted was that he saw Chris Saul sniffing coke in the men's washroom. Other than that, our Damian Palmer seems a decent enough type. He is a Professor of Creative Writing at Wilfrid Laurier University and a supposedly happily married man with two children and a house in Guelph."

DCI Parker interrupted Sergeant Flowers again, "Okay, Sergeant. What about the Books and Brunch, authors?"

Sergeant Flowers turned his typed sheet of paper over and began to read aloud, "Pippa Hargreaves, born in Toronto in 1981, trained as a nurse and still works part time at St. Joseph's hospital in Roncesvalles. She wrote her first Harlequin Romance novel when she was just eighteen, The Sins of Sexy Suzy, was a best seller and so she wrote ten more romances over the following fifteen years. She has been married twice.

"Actually, Pippa only checked into The Little Inn at 8:30 p.m. and regrettably missed The Crime Writers talk. She says that she was in bed by 9:30 exhausted after her drive from Toronto. She checked out at 2:30 p.m. the following day after the romance workshop. She said that she hadn't even met either Chris Saul or Damian Palmer and had not read any of their books.

"Now, Melissa Manson definitely knew Chris Saul, in fact, it was she who shared a bottle of wine with him in his room and also had sex with him. She said that he was incredibly sleepy and could barely rise to the occasion. She left him in his bed at around 12:30 sleeping like a baby and snoring like an elephant.

"Melissa has written over a dozen Harlequin romances. She says that she believes in love at first sight and felt that Chris and she were soul mates. She began to cry at this stage of the interview although I thought that the tears were for my benefit, and she was just being melodramatic. Finally, I interviewed the children's book author, Sally Albright. I have to say that she was a piece of work."

DCI Parker coughed and shot the Sergeant a look.

He cleared his throat and spoke. "Sorry, Ma'am, it's just that she was not the easiest of people to interview. Firstly, she refused to answer any questions and so I had to tell her that she was obliged by law to answer and if she didn't, she would be charged with obstructing the law. She reluctantly agreed to my questions.

Sally Albright was born in Manchester, England in 1981. She immigrated to Canada in 2005 and got a job working at DFI investments where none other than Chris Saul was also working. They married one year later but that marriage only lasted one year. In 2007 she wrote the first of the Cyril the Squirrel series and with good marketing the squirrel books became a television series, and our Sally made a fortune.

"She didn't know that her ex-husband Chris, was going to be a guest speaker at the festival, in fact, she had nothing nice to say about him although she conceded that the split up had been her decision. She had outgrown the man. One thing that she kept talking about was her new baby. I thought that she was referring to a real child until it came to me that she was actually talking about her latest creation, Molly the Mouse. The woman seemed unhinged to me, just a little strange to say the least. That's all I have, Ma'am." Sergeant Flowers sat down and removed his glasses, folding them up, and putting them in his shirt pocket.

DCI Parker stood up and walked over to the incident glass, a replacement for the old white board she was used to using. A large photograph of Chris Saul was taped to the centre of the glass. Susan had chosen a fluorescent green pen to write her notes. She handed the pen to Constable Ryan saying, "Here, Constable, you can scribe for me. "

"Okay, team, let's summarize what we know about the deceased. Firstly, he was born in Winnipeg in 1980. He studied maths at the University of Windsor, graduated in 2002, moved to Toronto, and worked with DFI investments as an advisor. Here he met Sally Albright and was married to her in 2006. Before that, in 2004, he had been made senior advisor for DFI at the ripe old age of twenty-four. The following year he wrote his first novel called, Money Matters, and it became a television hit. When he was twenty-six, he wrote the first of his Inspector Richardson series which also became an instant hit. By 2008 he had left DFI to concentrate on his writing. In 2012, Chris Saul married Jane White of Winnipeg, from his own home-town. He has two children, Hannah, six, and Neil, two. Oh, and he had written ten Inspector Richardson novels."

Susan paused a moment to let Constable Ryan catch up on her writing. She reviewed her notes, "Right, what connections do we have here, team?"

Constable Ryan put her hand up.

"Yes, Constable, what connections do you see?"

Constable Ryan blurted out, "Well, one obvious connection is his first marriage to Sally Albright, the children's author, Ma'am."

Susan took the pen from Constable Ryan and drew a line on the glass sheet connecting Chris Saul to Sally Albright.

"Are there anymore obvious connections?" Susan said.

Sergeant Flowers stood up. "Yes, well, both Sally Albright and Chris Saul worked for the same company DFI."

Susan wrote DFI, circled it, and drew lines from Chris and Sally to it.

Constable Elliot stood up, "Well, Damian Palmer and Chris Saul were both guest speakers on the same evening, plus they were witnessed having a fight in the bar that evening."

Susan wrote Damian Palmer's name on the glass and drew lines to Chris Saul.

"Anything else?" She said while staring at the glass.

Constable Brown stood up. "I don't know if they would be considered connected, but what about the witnesses to the argument at the bar?" He looked at his notes before continuing, "There were two witnesses, one a Doctor Glover and the other, Peggy Grierson. Oh, and the waiter and the barman were also witnesses."

Susan wrote their names on the glass under the heading, Witnesses.

Constable Brown continued, "There was also another witness, a Rose Blair, although she was not an eyewitness, she just heard the commotion from the hallway.

Susan smiled and thought to herself, of course, Rose would somehow be involved. Her friend always seemed to be in the right place, at the right time when it came to all the murders that had taken place in Bayfield.

Constable Ryan stood up again. "What about the Harlequin romance writer, Melissa Manson, she was the last person to see Chris Saul alive at 12:30 a.m. She is surely another connection?"

"Thank you, Constable Ryan," Susan said, "You pre-empted me. I was just going to raise the subject myself. The two people who stand out as our possible prime suspects are, number one, Damian Palmer and then, number two, this Melissa Manson. Also, I would not rule out Sally Albright. She might have been harbouring a grudge all these years against her ex-husband. You know what they say about a woman scorned. So, we need to dig deeper into all four of these suspects. They could all have motive for murder. Now, I want to talk about the means. Chris Saul was injected with a lethal dose of potassium chloride. Who would even have the knowledge or the ability to use a syringe?"

Sergeant Flowers said, "Someone with a medical background?"

"Exactly," Susan said, "and the only one of our suspects with a medical background is Pippa Hargreaves and she didn't even make the list of prime suspects. I'm going to add her to the list right now. So, Constable Elliot and Brown, your job is to dig deeper into Pippa Hargreaves' statement and, indeed, her life. Do not leave any stone unturned. Now Sergeant Flowers, I want you to interview Damian Palmer and Melissa Manson again. I want to know everything about them right down to their favourite colour. In other words, I want a thorough biography of both suspects."

Susan turned to Constable Ryan, "Constable, you are left with the ex-wife and somewhat eccentric Sally Albright. Once again, I want a thorough expo of the woman and everything that has happened to her in the past.

"Go to it, team. We'll meet back here tomorrow morning."

The team trickled out of The Lion's Hall leaving Susan to type up her report. She looked at her watch. It was almost lunch time. Maybe she would stop by The Black Dog and grab a bite to eat before going home. Peter might still be there. She would text him and suggest that he join her for lunch.

TEN

R ose and Tom had just waved goodbye to Jessica and the girls and were about to sit down to a nice cup of tea, when the telephone rang. It was Kate, Rose's sister.

"Oh, Rose," she barked down the phone, "I've managed to get a flight on West Jet. It leaves tomorrow and gets into London midday. Are you absolutely sure that you don't mind me coming to stay? I've got a return date for two weeks' time, but that can be changed easily."

Rose interrupted her sister. "Look Kate, I'm so looking forward to seeing you again and you can stay as long as you like. Have you spoken to Ally yet?"

There was a long silence before Kate answered, "No, I thought that it would be better if I spoke to her in person. She's such a daddy's girl. I'm not sure how she is going to react to the news."

"Look Kate, she will have to be told soon. How about I invite her over to dinner the day after tomorrow? I'll ask Paul if he could pick her up and drive her here. It's about time that we saw our son. It's been almost two months since he last visited us here in Bayfield."

"How is he doing? Did he ever get back together with that darling Japanese girl, Atsuko?"

"Oh, Kate, they've been separated for over a year and no, I'm sorry to say, they've both moved on. In fact, Paul was talking about a divorce last Christmas. It is so sad."

"Well, at least there are no children involved." Kate said once again sounding melancholy.

There was a short silence on the line and then Rose said brightly, "So, we'll see you tomorrow at the airport. Safe travelling. Love you, Kate."

Rose put the phone down. Tom, who had been clearing away the debris from their lunch, looked up and saw Rose looking pensive.

"Is everything alright, love?"

"Oh yes, everything's okay. Kate's coming tomorrow but she hasn't told Ally yet about Bob and Natalie. I'm not sure how she will take the news. She absolutely adores her dad."

Tom walked over to Rose and put his arms around her.

"You know, love, marriage split ups are so common these days. I bet Ally takes it all in her stride. You'll see, everything will work out alright, no need to fret."

"I'm not so sure, Tom. Remember how Ally suffered from anorexia when she was sixteen? I hope that this doesn't throw her backwards. Tom, do you still love me?"

Tom looked at Rose with disbelief. He kissed her tenderly and then said with a thick voice.

"You know that you are my whole world. I'll love you till the day I die. Do you remember that poem by Robert Browning?

Grow old with me
The best is yet to be...
Well, I want you and I to grow old together, forever.
Rose kissed Tom and said, "Oh, Tom, I love you too."

ELEVEN

D CI Susan Parker finished her lunch at The Black Dog and walked to her car. The village of Bayfield was still very quiet although with Easter only one week away it would soon wake up from its winters sleep.

Shops would open and there would be a renewed sense of revival down the Main Street. Susan had parked her car outside the new Japanese fusion restaurant called Drift.

It had opened late summer of the previous year and had already received good reviews. It could only seat sixteen inside the bar area, but in the summer the patio could hold up to thirty people.

The young man who owned the restaurant was both handsome and charming. He was a true entrepreneur and had moved to Bayfield after travelling around the world. I must book a table for four, Susan thought as she got into her car. It's about time I took Rose and Tom out for dinner.

Susan's car was parked right in front of the large wooden statue of Harry the Sailor. Wearing a bright yellow sou'wester, the sailor stood out incongruously. Susan drove down Main Street to The Little Inn and turned right onto Catherine Street and down to Bayfield Terrace. She was about to drive past Rose and Tom Blair's house when, on impulse, she pulled into their driveway and jumped out of her car.

The house always looked so charming even in winter, Susan thought as she knocked on the door and heard Puff and Ben bark in response. Tom opened the door and greeted Susan with a huge smile.

"Well, hello stranger," he said while holding Ben's collar trying to restrain the eager Labrador from jumping up and licking Susan to pieces.

"I was just passing by and thought that I hadn't seen you two in ages."

"Come on in, darling," Tom called out. "Susan's here." Susan entered and took off her boots.

Tom couldn't stop himself from admiring her shapely legs. He never would have credited his own behaviour as being attracted to Susan Parker, but there was just something about her that made him behave somewhat irrationally; rather like an adolescent teenager, yet he loved his wife dearly. It didn't make sense, but since when did sex ever follow any set rules of attraction?

"How lovely to see you, Susan," Rose said as she came into the lobby. "Come in and join us with a well-deserved drink. Jessica, Abby, and Ella have just left and I'm in need of some fortification." Rose laughed and went to give her friend a hug.

"So how are you? Enjoying being a Chief Inspector?"

Susan rolled her eyes. "You know something, Rose, I think that I'm crazy. I could be retired and sailing into the sunset by now, but instead I'm up to my eyes in paperwork. The bureaucracy and red tape, not to mention the meetings I have to deal with, is positively mind boggling!"

Rose led Susan into the sunroom. Ben and Puff followed, while Tom went to fix the drinks.

"Have you eaten? I've got some spaghetti pie and chocolate cake if you're hungry."

"Normally I'd jump at a piece of your cake, but I just ate fish 'n chips at The Black Dog. I wanted to ask if you would like to join Peter and I for dinner tonight at that new restaurant, Drift."

"That would be great. What time did you have in mind?" Rose said while handing Susan a glass of wine.

"Around 6:30 p.m. would be good. I tried to get hold of Peter earlier on, but he must have gone out. He did say something about going to Goderich. I'll have to confirm with him and make sure he doesn't have any other plans for tonight. I'll call you later on after I've spoken to him."

Rose smiled at her friend. It was so good to see her looking happy again. Two years previous her fiancé, Henri Le Bruin, had been shot and killed leaving Susan bereaved. She had spiralled into a deep depression, retired from the police force, and moved to Bayfield where Rose had gently tried to nurse her back to health.

"So, how is work? Are you investigating the death at The Little Inn by any chance?" Rose innocently asked.

"Oh, Rose Blair, you know darn well that I am. Knowing you, you're dying to hear all the details. I'm sorry to say we are slim on motive although we know the means. Remember, means, motive, and opportunity are the motto we live by."

"So, Chris Saul was murdered," Rose said incredulously. "I thought that he had died of a heart attack?"

"It was made to look like a heart attack, but he was actually injected with a dose of potassium chloride which gives the appearance of a heart attack. Traces of the chemical were found in his blood along with a strong sedative. You know, Rose, I shouldn't be telling you any of this, it's strictly police business."

"Well, Susan, I have to say I didn't like the man one single bit. I know you shouldn't talk ill of the dead, but he was particularly obnoxious. I overheard him laying into that nice author, Damian Palmer, after their readings. He was horrid to him and so arrogant and totally full of himself."

"Rose," Susan said, "you read a lot, what was Chris Saul's writing like?"

"Actually, I'm a great fan of his Inspector Richardson murder mysteries. They're all set in Winnipeg. Did he grow up there?"

"Yes, yes he did. But what about the other authors? Did you attend the Books and Brunch or the Children's Author's lunch?"

"Yes, I went to the Saturday morning workshop. Actually, I was there when the house maid found the body. She was terribly upset. Oh, and Jessica attended the Children's Author workshop this morning and said that Sally Albright was a real piece of work. She shouted at Ella and quite upset the book signing."

Susan interrupted Rose, "What about the Books and Brunch? How did you find those authors?"

"The romance writers were okay although I found the one author, Melissa Manson, somewhat irritating. She seemed very..." Rose never finished her sentence as Susan's cell phone rang.

"Detective Parker speaking." Susan said crisply.

Rose couldn't hear the other side of the conversation, but her ears pricked up when Susan said out aloud.

"Surely, I cannot believe it. Not another murder?"

Susan concluded her conversation and then turned to Rose. "I'm so sorry Rose, I have to leave. There's been another unexplained death at The Little Inn."

"Who is it this time?" Rose asked.

"Keep it under your hat, Rose, but the dead woman is none other than Sally Albright, the children's author."

"My gosh. I certainly didn't like the woman, but to hear that she's dead, wow, that's quite shocking."

"Anyway, I have to go. I hope that I can still make our dinner date tonight. I'll let you know if there are any changes in our plan."

Tom returned with a tray of drinks and a bowl of chips just as Susan was leaving the house.

"Where's she going?" he asked while putting the tray of drinks on the coffee table.

"Oh, Tom, there's been another death at The Little Inn. The author of Cyril the Squirrel is dead!"

TWELVE

When Susan arrived at The Little Inn, there was quite a commotion going on in the lobby. The manager was trying to calm down the housemaid who was visibly in distress. In fact, she was verging on being hysterical. It was, apparently the same girl who had discovered Chris Saul the previous day and the shock of finding yet a second victim had sent her into hysterics.

Susan went up to the manager and once again was amazed at her calmness and ethereal beauty.

"Can you tell me what happened?"

They walked into the dining room before talking so that guests of the Inn would not be privy to their conversation.

"Lydia went in to change the sheets and generally clean the room. Umm... Ms. Albright had requested a late checking out but had said that she would be leaving the Inn by 3:00 p.m. At 3:30 Lydia went upstairs and found Ms. Albright sprawled out on top of the bed fully dressed, obviously dead. I'll take you upstairs and you can see for yourself."

Susan followed the manager up the stairs and down the hallway past Chris Saul's room which still had yellow tape across the doorway, towards the back of the Inn. It was a smaller room than Chris's with a double bed in the middle and a shower room to the right of the doorway. Lying on the bed was Sally Albright still wearing the same taupe coloured suite and glossy stilettos. Her eyes were wide open and staring up at the ceiling, her mouth was open as if responding to a surprise. Death had been her surprise and by the looks of things it had come very much unexpectedly.

Susan made a few phone calls. The SOC team would have to be alerted and, of course, the medical examiner and pathologist, Dr. Green.

Outwardly there appeared no obvious signs of cause of death, but the similarity to the death of Chris Saul gave Susan pause for thought. Oh, God, please tell me that this isn't the work of a serial killer, she fervently prayed while surveying the scene of potential crime. Of course, the poor woman could have died of any number of natural causes, but the fact of the matter was the timing. It just seemed too much of a coincidence that the two deaths should both have taken place at The Little Inn where both of the deceased were guest speakers.

To her surprise, Dr. Green, or Ian as he insisted on being called, appeared in the doorway just five minutes later.

"Boy, that was quick," Susan said. "How did you drive from Goderich to Bayfield in five minutes?"

"Ah, when you phoned I was actually just sitting down to a late lunch at The Albion. I'd been visiting my aunt earlier. She lives on Jane Street. Okay, so who do we have here?" Ian walked into the room and stood looking down at the victim lying on the bed.

"Her name is Sally Albright. She was one of the authors at The Literary Festival. I believe that she wrote the Cyril the Squirrel series."

"Oh, my nephew James has the whole collection. What a shame. I guess there will be no more Cyril books now."

"Umm.... yes, well, I'll leave you to your work. Please let me know as soon as possible if you suspect foul play."

Ian pulled out of his black leather case a white body suit, latex gloves, and blue booties. He turned to Susan and gave her a huge, toothy smile.

"Well, it's good to see you again, Detective Parker. I'll be in touch the minute I have an idea of the cause of death. Will you be around if I want to get hold of you?"

"Yes, I've already set up an incident room at The Lion's Hall and that's where I'm heading right now. Call me if you find anything, and I mean anything, suspicious about this death."

Susan left the room and went downstairs. Ian, or Dr. Green, was a funny fellow, one minute he was all business and the next she was convinced he had been coming on to her. She wondered whether he was single and, with that thought in mind, she texted Peter.

Where r u?

Almost instantly he replied.

I'm at your place.

Susan looked at her watch. It was already 4:30 p.m. There was no point in calling in her team until they knew if they were dealing with another murder or not. I might as well go home, Susan thought as she opened the lobby door and stepped outside to where she had left her car.

THIRTEEN

Rose looked at her watch. It was 4:30 p.m. and she still hadn't heard from Susan.

"I wonder if dinner is still on with Susan and Peter tonight." She said to Tom who was buried behind the newspaper with both dogs curled up, one each side of him, on the sofa.

"Did you say something, darling?" Tom muttered behind his paper.

"Oh, it doesn't matter," Rose said irritably. Sometimes Tom drove her mad. He really had selective hearing, plus the fact that he actually wasn't hearing too well these days but refused to acknowledge the fact. The joys of getting older, Rose thought for the umpteenth time.

The telephone suddenly rang, and Rose called out. "Speak of the devil. That must be Susan now."

But it wasn't, it was Peggy Grierson, the Chair of the Town Hall Committee.

"Hello, Rose. I'm just phoning to remind you of our next meeting this Tuesday. You can still make it I hope?"

Rose had in fact completely forgotten about it.

"Oh… yes, I can be there, but I won't be able to stay too long as my sister Kate will be here. She arrives tomorrow from Kelowna."

"Well, I promise to make the meeting brief. We don't have too much on the agenda. Did you enjoy the Literary Festival? I saw Tom and you last Friday night, but I didn't see you today at the children's authors' workshop and brunch? Although I think that I saw your daughter Jessica in the audience."

"So, you attended the Children's Author workshop, Peggy. I hate to be the bearer of sad news, but Sally Albright, the author of Cyril the Squirrel, is dead."

There was a stunned silence on the other end of the line.

"Well, I never," Peggy exclaimed. "I knew about the crime writer's death. What was his name again?"

"Chris Saul," Rose said.

"Yes, Chris Saul. Well, Dr. Glover and I were interviewed by the police, so we were aware of his passing, but Sally Albright. That's quite shocking. I mean I didn't really like the woman, but…"

Rose looked at her watch again. She liked Peggy dearly, but she could go on and on and right now she was in no mood for gossip.

"Peggy, I really must go now as I'm expecting a call. I'll see you on Tuesday. Bye now."

Rose put the phone down and stared at the wall. It really was quite bizarre that two out of the five authors attending the literary festival, should now be dead.

Her reverie was interrupted by the shrill ringing tone of the telephone. Surely this time it must be Susan, Rose thought as she picked up the phone. It was Paul, their son, phoning from London.

"Mom, I've just had a call from Ally. She says that her mother is flying over for a visit. She asked if I would drive her to Bayfield to visit her mom. What about Tuesday evening? Would that work for you?"

"Why yes, how lovely, we'll get to see both you and Ally at the same time. We haven't seen either of you for ages. How is everything going, darling?"

Paul went quiet before answering.

"Well, teaching is fine, but not so good on the relationship front. Mom, I might go back to Japan for a bit. Atsuko's going through a rough time right now. Her dad just died, and she's taken his death very badly."

"Oh, I'm so sorry to hear that. He seemed in good health when we saw him at your wedding, but I suppose that was almost five years ago now. What did he actually die from?"

"I think that it was something to do with the liver. He was a heavy drinker."

"Well, I am very sorry indeed. I must send the family our condolences. Anyhow, Paul, I'm hoping that Ally and you will stay for dinner. What time should we expect you both?"

"Around 5ish, Mom. My lectures finish at 3:00 pm and I think that Ally said that she was free from 2:30 onwards. I'll pick her up around 3:30 and drive straight on to Bayfield."

"Great. We so look forward to seeing you again. See you soon, love."

It was only after she had put the phone down that Rose remembered the Town Hall committee meeting. She would have to give her apologies to Peggy. Family always should come first, she thought thinking about her sister and all the problems that lay ahead.

FOURTEEN

When Susan got back to the Harbour Court condo's she literally bumped into Peter who was just stepping out of the house with all his photographic gear slung over his shoulder.

"Where are you going?" Susan asked and then she bit her tongue. "Ah, sorry Peter, of course, you've got work to do. I've just come from The Little Inn. How long do you think you'll be as I've asked Rose and Tom to join us for dinner at Drift at 6:30 p.m.?"

Peter looked at his watch. It was already 4:45 pm. "It shouldn't take too long, maybe thirty minutes. I'll be back in time for pre-dinner drinks. See you later."

With that, Peter gave Susan a quick kiss on her cheek and went to get his car.

Susan watched as he drove off in his black Porsche. She really wasn't sure where their relationship was heading. It made her uncomfortable not knowing. Making herself a cup of coffee, Susan threw off her shoes and plonked herself down in front of the television and was just enjoying watching the news when the phone rang. It was Ian Green, the pathologist.

"Hi, Susan, Ian Green here. Look, I've just found something interesting. I think that you should come over and see for yourself. I'm fairly certain that we're looking at murder."

Susan sighed and said that she would be over in five minutes.

Room 14 at The Little Inn was exactly as Susan had left it although now there were four SOC technicians all wearing white suits and sporting disposable booties. Yellow tape cordoned off the doorway and a police officer stood outside to guard the room. Peter had set up his tripod and lights and was busy bending over the body taking a close up of Sally Albright. Dr. Green was engaged in talking to one of the SOC team members.

"So, what have you got to show me, Ian?" Susan asked anxiously.

"Of course, what I tell you now will not stand up in court so you will have to verify all of this later on for the official report of the cause of death, but just look here." He pointed to a small dot on the side of Sally's neck, just under her chin. "You see this puncture mark, well, it's in the exact same place that I found a puncture mark on Chris Saul's body. Of course, toxicology will have to prove that both injections were administered by the same person. In other words, Sally Albright likely was given a dose of potassium chloride just like Chris Saul. I hate to tell you this, but it looks like we have a serial killer on our hands."

Susan's heart sank. She knew just how difficult it was to catch a serial killer. Remembering a case she had worked on when she was a mere rookie Constable over thirty years ago, Susan recalled how it had taken the team two years to find the killer. By then he'd murdered six people. Well, six that had been found. He had claimed to have killed twenty. It had been a nightmare. Susan inadvertently shuddered and wrapped her arms around herself as if she was cold.

"Are you alright, Detective?" Ian asked as he read the thermometer in his hand.

"Yes, I'm fine, just had bad memories of another serial killer on the rampage. What time of death do you have for us, Doctor?"

Ian looked at the thermometer again and shook his head, "I would say that she's only been dead a couple of hours at most. Her body was still warm when I got here. It's cooling down quite rapidly now. Let's see, she probably died around 2:30 p.m. or so, maybe 3:00 p.m. She was found at around 3:40, which was cutting it rather fine for our killer."

Susan thanked him and went to leave the room, but not before quietly speaking to Peter who was in the middle of putting away his equipment.

"I don't think that we'll be able to have dinner with Tom and Rose tonight. Could you swing by and give them my apology? I have to call in the team as we definitely have another murder on our hands."

"Okay, look, I'll cook us a curry or something. We can eat that when you get in. See you later."

Dr Green looked over at Susan and Peter and said, "Are you two an item then?"

Susan just smiled and left the room to call up her team. They had a lot of work to do, and time was clicking by.

FIFTEEN

The team had all gathered in The Lion's Hall by six o'clock. Amazingly nobody had grumbled at being called out on their day off as they all knew that murder waited for nobody.

Susan stood up and pointed to the investigation glass where she had glued a picture of Chris Saul. She had managed to print off a picture of Sally Albright taken from her publicist brochure. This she added to the glass.

"Listen up everybody. We have what potentially could be a serial killer loose in the village. Two murders with the exact same profile are just too much of a coincidence to be anything but the same killer. We are waiting for the toxicology and blood results back from the pathologist and I am ninety-five percent sure that we will find Sally Albrights death caused from an injection of potassium chloride. Now why have these two victims been singled out? We need to investigate their backgrounds and see if we can find any possible connections."

Constable Ryan put her hand up. Susan looked at her sternly, she hated to be interrupted.

"Yes, Constable Ryan, what is it?"

Constable Ryan stood up nervously. "The obvious, ma'am, is that Sally and Chris were once married." She looked at her notes and continued, "They were married in 2007 and divorced in 2008." She sat down again.

"Thank you," Susan said, "Yes, I'm well aware of that and it is a big connection, but it doesn't get us any closer to knowing why the killer wanted this couple dead. Is there anything else that connects these two people?"

There was silence in the room and then Constable Ryan put her hand up again.

Susan said dryly, "Yes, Constable Ryan, what else have you found for us?"

"Well, Ma'am, they both worked at DFI as financial advisors. I think that is where they met each other. That's another connection, isn't it?"

"Okay, thanks Constable Ryan. We need to look into this DFI and to dig deeper into Sally Albright and Chris Saul's pasts."

Sergeant Flowers raised his hand. "Ma'am, if we are dealing with a serial killer might he not have killed before?"

Susan nodded thoughtfully. "Yes, that's a good point, Sergeant, you're quite right. Okay, here's what I want you to do. Sergeant Flowers, your task is to check the archives of the cold cases and unsolved murders. Look out particularly for our killer's signature, unexplained heart attacks, or evidence of injections of potassium chloride.

"Constable Ryan and Brown, I want you to dig up as much information as you can on this DFI Finance Company with emphasis on the years that Chris Saul and Sally Albright were employed. Constable Elliot, your task is to find where our killer could have had access to potassium chloride."

Constable Ryan put her hand up again. Really, Susan thought, her eagerness was becoming quite irritating. She, however, said, "Yes, Constable, what is it now?"

"Ma'am, I beg your pardon, but surely the only person with

reasonable access to syringes and drugs would either be a nurse or a doctor. It would certainly have to be someone with a medical background."

Constable Elliot who had remained quiet throughout the briefing put his hand up. "Ma'am, Pippa Hargreaves is a nurse."

There was an excited hum in the room as the team digested this piece of information.

"Okay, Constable Elliot, you can also look into Pippa Hargreaves past and while you're at it, do another check on Melissa Manson. She was, after all, the last person to have seen Chris Saul alive. Now, Damian Palmer, where does he stand in all of this? He claims to have been asleep when Chris Saul was murdered, and, according to The Little Inn, he had checked out by lunch time after we had finished interviewing him. I think that we should speak to him again and I'll go and do that myself. Right, go to it team and bring me back some results."

They all filed out of The Lion's Hall leaving Susan to type up her report. She looked at her watch. It was only 7:00 p.m., they could have still gone out to dinner, but by now Peter would have made his curry and it would be too late to call Rose and Tom. Oh, well, another evening would have to do. Susan closed her laptop and headed for home.

SIXTEEN

Rose felt quite excited. She hadn't seen her sister Kate for over a year, and she was very fond of her. Although there was only four years between them, Rose had always felt very protective towards her baby sister. Now that Kate was coming to visit, she was determined to make sure her stay was good if only to take her sister's mind off Bob's unfaithfulness.

Whenever she thought about Kate's husband, Rose's blood boiled. How could he leave her lovely sister, particularly for Natalie? Kate was the model wife, the ultimate super mom, and everything any man could ever aspire to have in a partner. How dare Bob go off with Natalie? What did Natalie have that Kate did not?

Rose tried to recall if she had ever met Natalie so that she could put a face to the name. She had certainly heard about her over the years. Kate's children were the same ages as Natalie's.

They had carpooled together for years when living in Kelowna. That was before they had moved out to the hobby farm.

Thinking of the farm gave Rose further pause for thought. Who would look after the livestock while Kate was away? If Bob moved to Penticton to be with Natalie that would leave the farm untended.

Oh, well, Rose thought, I'm sure that Kate's got it all sorted out. Tom interrupted her train of thought.

"Darling, are you ready? We really should be on the road soon if we're to get to the airport on time."

Rose looked at her watch. It was already 10:30 and it would take at least an hour to drive to the airport. Kate's flight was due to arrive at 12:00. They would most certainly have to leave soon.

"Do we have time to take the dogs for a quick walk, Tom?" Rose said anxiously as she hated to leave Puff and Ben cooped up all day without a walk.

"Well, love, I suppose a quick once around the block would be okay. Do you want me to come with you?"

"No, it's alright. I'll be just ten minutes." Rose got the leashes down from the hook on the back of the laundry door. She grabbed some plastic bags and was out of the door being pulled by two very excited dogs all within five minutes. Tom waved to her from the front window.

Rose walked quickly down Bayfield Terrace towards Pioneer Park, but when she got to Catherine Street she decided to turn left and then left again onto Colina Street.

As she walked past Lynda Forbes house, she noticed Peggy Grierson with Doctor Glover standing in front of her friend's house. They had Peggy's little fox terrier, Lucy on a leash and had obviously been taking her for a walk. Puff and Ben practically dragged Rose over in their haste to greet Lucy who snarled at them and held her ground with a ferocious growl. Rose pulled the dogs to heel and told them off. "Oh, do behave you two. That's enough now."

Rose turned to them and said, "Good morning Peggy and Doctor Glover. I'm so glad that I bumped into you. I was going to send you an email because I cannot make the Town Hall meeting tomorrow. My sister's daughter, Ally and our son, Paul, are coming to dinner tomorrow night. I completely forgot about it when I last spoke to you on the phone."

Peggy's face dropped, but she had the courtesy to be gracious to Rose, "Oh, I'm sorry about that. I do hope that we still have a quorum, you know what it's like this time of year as not all the snow-birds have returned. But still, don't you worry. How long is your sister staying?"

Rose was anxious to get away from Peggy. She did like to talk.

"Oh, she's here for a fortnight. I must dash now. Enjoy your walk. Bye."

Rose tugged at the leashes and pulled Ben and Puff abruptly away from the snarling Lucy. Walking briskly, she continued her circuit back to their house. Tom was standing by the car, keys in hand, and looking impatiently at his watch.

"I'll just put the dogs in the house and then we can leave." Rose said and within minutes had joined Tom. They were soon on their way to pick up Kate from the airport.

SEVENTEEN

Susan did some of her best thinking when on the open road, particularly on the peaceful country roads of Huron County where she barely saw another car in sight. She thought about the serial killer and why he or she would want to murder two of the authors from the Literary Festival. Just what was the common connection between Sally Albright and Chris Saul other than the obvious fact that they were both authors, successful ones at that.

Another connection was the fact that they had once been married, all but briefly. Then there was the other connecting factor, and that was where they had first met at the financial advisory group known as DFI in Toronto. Hopefully her team would be able to garner some more background material which might point them in the right direction of the killer or, at the very least, give them some sense of the motive behind the murders.

She arrived at her destination a couple of hours later which was the campus of Wilfred Laurier in Guelph. Trying to find a parking space proved one huge nightmare.

Since when did so many students own cars? She thought while

finally finding a narrow parking space sandwiched behind a dumpster and a couple of motor bikes.

Susan walked through the main entrance of the building and went to the reception desk. She was about to ask the rather harried looking woman working behind a computer where to find Professor Damian Palmer, when she saw a sign overhead pointing the way to the Creative Writing department. Susan followed the arrows and soon found herself in a small wing of the main building.

As luck would have it, Damian Palmer's office was immediately on the right as she entered the department. Susan had phoned him that morning before setting off from Bayfield and he had said that he would be free to talk as he had no lectures on a Monday, just a load of administrative work to catch up on. He had agreed to meet her at 10:00 a.m. Susan looked at her watch and it was 9:50 a.m., perfect timing, she thought as she knocked on the door.

Damian Palmer opened the door. He was a good-looking man, much younger than Susan had expected. His hair was a pale brown and was worn short at the sides and thicker on top. He had intense, intelligent green eyes and a warm welcoming smile.

"You must be Detective Inspector Parker."

Before Susan could stop herself, she corrected him. "Actually, it's Detective Chief Inspector Parker," and then she could have bitten her tongue off as Damian Palmer looked suitably abashed.

"So sorry, Detective Chief Inspector, would you like to come in?"

He led the way into a small, rather messy office where books lay everywhere in a general state of disarray. Damian could see Susan looking at the mess. He quickly said, "Don't mind the chaos. I'm clearing out half of these books. The only trouble is trying to select the ones that I want to keep. So, how can I help you? I did give a statement to one of your officers on Saturday before I left the Inn."

Susan got out her notebook and pen. She started to say, "Mr. Palmer."

Which he quickly interjected, "Just call me Damian. Mr. Palmer seems so formal and rather intimidating."

"Damian, I just have a few further questions to ask you. Firstly, where were you on Sunday afternoon?"

He looked suitably confused. "Well, I was home with my wife and family here in Guelph. But why are you asking?"

Susan continued without a beat. "Can you verify that you were in Guelph? We do need to have proof of your alibi."

"Yes, you can ask my wife and children. We stayed in all day yesterday. I needed to relax after my busy Friday, and I had a ton of papers to mark. It's the end-of-year exams and I'm on a deadline to get the marks out. Are you going to tell me what this is all about?"

Susan thought about it for a minute and then replied. "There has been another murder at The Little Inn. Sally Albright, the author of Cyril the Squirrel, was found dead in her room yesterday afternoon."

Damian looked really shocked, "Wow, two murders in one weekend. I shouldn't think that the owners of The Little Inn will be feeling too happy. Murder could be bad for business, or maybe not. The pundits also say, any publicity, good or bad, is good for business, so take your pick."

"Did you know Sally Albright at all?" Susan asked.

"No, I didn't, although I know of the Cyril books. My daughter Claire has a whole collection of them in her bedroom."

Susan tapped her notebook thoughtfully and said, "Another question I have for you... what exactly was your fight with Chris Saul really about? According to your statement you said that he accused you of mentioning a farm in Alliston in one of your books, the same farm that he had used in one of his Inspector Richardson novels, and he accused you of plagiarism, is that right?"

Damian grimaced at the memory. "Well, yes, Chris did accuse me of plagiarism, but it wasn't so much about using the name of the farmhouse in Alliston as the fact that he reckoned that I had taken great chunks of dialogue directly out of the 1979 movie, Love at First

Bite. He maintained that I used it word for word in my spoof novel, Suck it and See."

Susan laughed, "I remember that movie. It had George Hamilton and Susan St. James in it. It actually was very funny. But did you use parts of the movie in your book?"

Damian looked briefly annoyed, and his handsome face clouded over. He then let out a big sigh. "You know something, I didn't deliberately plagiarize anything. I wrote the novel as part of a creative writing exercise and never intended for it to be published. Yes, I had seen Love at First Bite, and maybe on a sub-conscious level I was influenced by it. But outward plagiarism of someone else's work, no way, of course not."

"So, why was Chris Saul so angry with you?"

Damian paused before answering Susan. "I don't really know apart from the obvious reason and that was that he was jealous. You see, in his eyes I had made it so big with my Suck It and See being made into a movie and all the subsequent spin-offs. I just put it down to professional jealousy, which sadly happens a lot in this business."

"Is there anything else that you can tell me about Chris Saul? Had you ever met before?"

"Well, yes, we had met before, but not as writers. About eight years ago I went to a company called DFI. They're financial advisors in Toronto, anyway, I sought advice on what to do with some inheritance money. My grandma had died and left me about $30,000. Chris Saul was working for DFI at that time."

Another connection Susan thought as she continued to question Damian. "So, did he advise you financially? What happened?"

Damian laughed and then frowned as his handsome face creased up into a grimace. "Well, I'm sure glad that I didn't take his advice. He strongly advised me to put my $30,000 into Nortel stocks. He said that they were a sure bet. I didn't go with him as he just seemed a bit overly pushy. Thank goodness though as by the end of that year it was all over with Nortel. Some people lost a mint."

"Was that the last time you saw him?" Susan asked while looking down at her watch. She would have to be leaving soon if she was to make her team meeting at 2:00 p.m.

"I saw him a couple of years ago when I was on a book signing tour. We were both staying at the same hotel in Kingston. He actually came up to congratulate me on my success and asked if I'd like to join him at a restaurant that he had discovered called, Chez Piggy.

"Well, did you go with him to the restaurant?" Susan knew Chez Piggy well. It had become almost something of an icon in Kingston having been there for years. She had fond memories of eating there way back in her student days.

"Actually, no, I had to decline as I had already agreed to eat out with my editor."

"So why was he so angry and accusatory with you the other night?" Susan said as she got up preparing to leave.

"Your guess is as good as mine." Damian said as he opened the door to her and held out his hand to shake hers.

"If there is anything else that you remember about Chris Saul, please do not hesitate to call me." Susan said as she handed Damian her business card.

During the drive back to Bayfield Susan couldn't stop thinking about her conversation with Damian Palmer, particularly the bit about his potential investment with DFI and the Nortel shares. Maybe, just maybe, there was something there, some link to the murder.

EIGHTEEN

From the minute that Tom and Rose greeted Kate at the arrivals in London Airport, until they finally got back to Bayfield over an hour later, she hadn't stopped talking.

Rose could see by the expression on Tom's face that he was struggling to stop himself from saying something that he would most certainly regret later. Rose loved her sister dearly, but even she was driven to distraction by her voice. The trouble was that Kate had an exceptionally loud and grating voice giving the impression of a very bossy person when in actuality Kate was a gentle, warm-hearted woman. Rose had often wondered if her sister was slightly deaf which could account for the loud voice or maybe she had just inherited the bark. Their grandma had also had an extremely strong and imperious voice.

They arrived back in Bayfield just in time for a late lunch. Rose had prepared an apple and squash soup before they had set off for London which she had left in a slow cooker. She had also made some fresh multigrain artisan bread the night before.

Puff and Ben greeted them effusively at the front door with their tails wagging and their great tongues lolling. Kate loved animals and the dogs could sense her affection for them.

"Come on puppies, come and join me on the sofa." Kate barked after she had been shown into the sunroom and been given instructions to relax while Rose made some tea and Tom made his escape to do goodness knows what in the garden.

With a little peace to herself, Rose checked her messages. There was a call from her dear friend, Lynda Forbes and one from Susan Parker, her two best friends in the village.

Rose phoned Lynda first. It was answered right away.

"Lynda Forbes speaking."

"Hi, Lynda, it's Rose."

"Oh, Rose, I was hoping that you'd get back to me soon. Look, we've got some friends coming for dinner tonight and I wondered if Tom and you might like to join us?"

"Oh, Lynda, we would love to, but my sister Kate has just arrived from out West."

"No problem, just bring her too. I would love to meet her."

"That's very kind of you. Yes, then, we would love to join you tonight. What time?"

"How about around 7:00 p.m. Great! Well, I'll see you later."

Rose put the phone down and concentrated on making the tea. She would phone Susan later.

Kate drank her tea and then wolfed down two bowls of squash soup and three slices of artisan bread. There certainly was nothing wrong with her appetite, Rose thought as she cleared away their lunch. Up until then Kate had not mentioned Bob or indeed anything about their marriage. She was undecided whether to let sleeping dogs lie or to confront the elephant in the room. In the end it was Tom who blurted out rather tactlessly, "Well, Kate, what's this all about between Bob and you?"

Rose looked aghast as Kate's lips quivered and her eyes began to well up with large, glistening tears.

"Oh, Tom, I wish that you could knock some sense into Bob's head. Right now, he is convinced that he loves my friend Natalie and that he hasn't loved me for years. It's that part that hurts me the most."

Kate began to cry, and Rose's heart could almost break with sadness for her poor sister.

"Maybe it's just a temporary fling thing," Rose said trying to lighten the atmosphere in the room.

"He's off his rocks," Tom added as he left the room.

Rose could see that he felt decidedly uncomfortable with the conversation, and she couldn't blame him although it was he who had opened up the can of worms.

She sought to change the subject. "Look, Kate, it's beautiful outside, let's take the dogs for a walk and get some fresh air."

Kate got up, blew her nose loudly and wiped her eyes with the back of her hand. She was one of those people that looked good crying, not like me, Rose thought, who went red and blotchy all over her face after crying.

Puff and Ben were really excited at the prospect of a walk. They could barely keep still enough to have their leashes attached to their collars. Rose and Kate left Tom who had shut himself away in the sunroom and was now buried behind a newspaper. They would at least be able to give him an hour's peace before returning home.

It truly was a beautiful April day and Spring was most certainly in the air. Daffodils were almost ready to flower and the crocuses too. Little delicate snow drops silently nodded their heads in the breeze as Rose and Kate walked down the road toward Pioneer Park.

"After we've taken the dogs for a walk down to the beach, we'll drop them back home and then I'm going to treat you to a drink at The Little Inn. I want you to meet the new owner and see what she's done to the place."

"But I loved it just the way it was," Kate said. She hadn't visited

Bayfield in at least five years and most certainly had not seen the changes to the Inn which had taken place a few years ago.

The dogs charged down the wooden steps and on to the sandy beach. There was not a single soul on the shores of Lake Huron. Driftwood had collected in piles on the beach left over from the winter storms and Ben grabbed a piece and started to drag it into the water. Kate laughed and ran after the frisky Labrador trying to pull the stick out of his mouth. The lake looked azure blue and absolutely picture perfect.

Although Rose just knew that the water would be icy, it almost looked tempting enough to take off her shoes and to paddle. Certainly, the temperature did not put Ben and Puff off from wading into the water. They were both incorrigible when it came to the lake. Nothing could stop them from charging in and then rushing out shaking their furry coats like crazy in an attempt to get dry.

Soon it was just too cold to stay near the water any longer. Rose and Kate leashed the dogs and dragged them reluctantly up the steps to Pioneer Park and then onto Bayfield Terrace and back home.

Tom was asleep on the sofa when they returned. Rose woke him up and gave him a towel to dry the dogs down while she and Kate rushed off again.

As they walked past Lynda Forbes' house Rose pointed it out to her sister.

"You'll see inside tonight as we've been invited over for dinner. Lynda is great, you'll love her, she is just one of those multi-talented people that you'd love to hate but can't because she's so nice. On top of everything else, she is probably the best cook that I know."

"I hate the woman already." Kate smiled, "but she has one interesting house. It looks a bit like an arts and crafts house or a Frank Lloyd Wright design."

Rose looked at Lynda's house again. Yes, her sister had a point, it did look like an art deco style of a home. Kate had studied art at Emily Carr in Vancouver many years ago and had started up her career as an art teacher before she had met Bob. After they were married, the children came quickly and Kate never went back to her teaching career. Maybe, Rose thought, she could resume her job at some level or go back to school again.

They arrived at The Little Inn. It was 4:00 p.m. and very quiet. The main street looked pretty dead which was normal for that time of year. Only the Bayfield General Store and a couple of other shops appeared to be open.

"Gosh, Rose, it's like a ghost town. Where on earth is everybody?" Kate asked as she looked down the deserted Main Street.

"Well, for a start it's a Monday, and it's always quiet at the beginning of the week in off season. But you know, an awful lot of people disappear south for the winter. It gets busier after Easter and then it's just ridiculously crazy in the summer."

They walked into the lobby of The Little Inn. Rose poked her head around into the tap room. Joanne, the owner was sitting up on one of the bar stools drinking a cup of coffee. She looked up and waved to Rose.

"Hi! come and join me for a cup of coffee."

"Joanne, this is my sister Kate." Rose said as they pulled up some stools and joined her at the bar. "Actually, we're going to have a glass of wine, do you want one too?"

"Oh, no, but thank you all the same." Joanne said before being interrupted by one of her staff.

"Excuse me, Joanne, but Lydia has not reported for duty. Do you want me to cover for her?"

"Yes, if you don't mind." Joanne said, and she then turned to Rose and Kate.

"Lydia found Sally Albright and Chris Saul and she was understandably upset. Actually, Dr. Glover and Peggy Grierson just happened to be here last Sunday having lunch. Lydia was hysterical. The doctor had to administer a sedative to calm her down. The poor girl, it was such a shock for her discovering two dead bodies. I do hope that she manages to return to work again as she is one of my best workers."

Kate looked at Rose with wide eyes. "Rose, my dear sister, don't tell me that you're involved with another murder in Bayfield?"

Rose laughed, "Actually, there have been two murders and no, I'm not involved with either of them although I just happened to be here on the Saturday morning when Lydia found Chris Saul in his bedroom. Jessica went to the Children's Authors workshop on Sunday which was run by Sally Albright. She was the woman found dead upstairs in her room."

Rose turned to Joanne and said, "Honestly, this can't be good for business."

Joanne looked thoughtful before she slowly replied. "Well, you would think that two murders taking place here would really put people off coming, but I think that it's done the opposite. Our bookings are up by fifty percent, and we have had special requests to stay in rooms 14 and 3, the two rooms where the murders took place."

"Oh.... how ghoulish," Kate said, "By the way, the changes that you've made are great. I loved The Little Inn the way it was before, but you've given it a more sophisticated look."

Joanne smiled and then looked over towards the door where Dr. Glover and Peggy Grierson were entering the room arm in arm, deep in conversation.

"Do they come here often?" Rose asked Joanne.

"Yes, most days. They come for a pre-dinner drink and sometimes they stay on for supper."

Rose smiled at Peggy and waved her fingers. It was good to see her looking happy again. She had been sad for so long after her husband had passed away. Dr. Glover had also been widowed for over eight years. It was great that the two of them had found a deep friendship at their age and stage of their lives. Loneliness was an awful affliction and plagued too many people. In the village of Bayfield alone Rose knew of dozens of lonely people. She shuddered at the thought of being without her beloved Tom. She wondered how she would cope. I would outwardly cope just fine, Rose thought uncomfortably, but inwardly I would slowly die of heartache.

Rose shook her head and said, "Right, well, we should be getting back. Tom will be wondering where we've got to."

They turned to leave and then Rose paused and asked Joanne one more question, "Do you know if Sally Albright died the same way as Chris Saul?"

Joanne nodded, "Why, yes. They both died the same way. I believe a lethal dose of potassium chloride was injected, and that gave an impression of a heart attack."

Kate looked suitably aghast and tugged at Rose's sleeve, "We really should get back before it gets dark. All this talk of death is making me feel creepy."

NINETEEN

The team was gathered and waited for DCI Parker to arrive. They chatted amongst themselves and were all in deep conversation when Susan rushed into the room.

"So sorry I'm late. I got here as soon as I could. There were road works just outside Mitchell and I got held up for ten minutes. Right, let's hope you've all got information that might move this case along. Let's start with you Sergeant Flowers, how did you get on with sifting through the cold cases?"

Sergeant Flowers stood up and unfolded his notes and began to read out loud.

"There were several cases of lethal injection, but only two where potassium chloride was used. One in 2011, a Jim Kidd and another only two years ago in 2015, a Matt Irons. I looked for common connections and found something pretty interesting. Both victims had worked for DFI in Toronto from 2005 to 2008. Sally Albright and Chris Saul also worked for DFI during that same time."

The Sergeant sat down.

Susan smiled and for the first time looked genuinely pleased.

"Wow, that's our first huge break through. Well done, Sergeant.

So, all the victims were connected by where they worked. Constables Ryan and Brown, what did you find out about DFI?"

Both Constables stood up. Constable Brown took the lead. "Well, ma'am, Design Finance Investments was founded in 1995. From what I can gather people seek advice from financial specialists who put together portfolios of short and long-term investment opportunities. Stocks, shares, and sometimes commodities. Basically, it's like a form of gambling by trying to get the biggest return for your money. Anyway, DFI are one of many similar organizations throughout the world. Wall Street market is at the top end and most financial advisors key into the daily ups and downs of stocks and shares. Sometimes investors make a lot of money, other times they lose big time. There is always a risk involved, it just depends how much people are prepared to gamble. In 2008 after the Nortel crash, many people lost a ton of money. Financial advisors like DFI came into a lot of grief when their clients lost their investments. It appears that Sally Albright and Chris Saul left DFI shortly after the crash, in fact, by 2010, none of the existing staff remained."

Susan interrupted Constable Brown, "So, who were the staff employed during the Nortel scandal?"

Constable Ryan thumbed through her notes on her iPad.

"Ah, here, I have it ma'am," she said and began reading out aloud. "Sally Albright, Chris Saul, James Kidd, Matt Irons, and a Lynda Barnes."

Susan interjected again, "So we have all four out of the five employees of DFI murdered by lethal injection. What about this fifth employee, Lynda Barnes? Could she possibly be the next victim? Constables Ryan and Brown, find her as soon as possible as she might be in mortal danger. Okay, Constable Elliot, let's have your report on Pippa Hargreaves. What did you find out about her?"

Constable Elliot stood up, wiped his brow, coughed, and then read from his notes written in a small note pad which he removed from his jacket pocket.

"Pippa Hargreaves was born in Toronto in 1981. She grew up in the Rosedale area and lived on Stanton Road near Crawley Park. She attended the local high school, graduated and then trained as a nurse, married a John Sutton in 2004, and worked as a nurse at St. Joseph's hospital. She divorced John in 2010 and wrote her first Harlequin romance in 2011. Pippa has written ten romances. She obviously would have access to syringes, but the hospital has very strict guidelines for pharmaceutical prescriptions. In other words, it would be very difficult for Pippa to get hold of potassium chloride unless it was prescribed specifically for a patient. That's all I have to report on Pippa Hargreaves, ma'am."

"Thank you, Constable. Okay, now in summary." Susan moved to the glass incident board and began to write as she spoke.

"Our biggest break through and connecting factor is that our two victims, Sally Albright and Chris Saul, worked for DFI at the same time as James Kidd and Matt Irons who were also victims of the same lethal injection making their murder profile the same as the others. Four out of the five staff members who were working for DFI during the period of 2006 to 2008, are now dead. There is a fifth staff member, a Lynda Barnes, still not accounted for. She, too, was part of the DFI team working there between 2006 and 2008."

Susan paused, put her pen down, and turned to the team.

"My hypothesis is that all of our victims were part of the collateral damage following the Nortel share collapse of 2008. Sally left DFI just before the crash, Chris Saul, the year after, and Matt and James both resigned just after the Nortel disaster. So, let's see, we have four victims all connected through DFI and the Nortel collapse. Now, our serial killer has murdered the victims over a period of five years starting with James Kidd in 2011."

Susan counted the victims with her fingers holding up her hand as she spoke their names.

"Matt Irons in 2015, and then two years later, Sally Albright and Chris Saul. We have the means, the lethal injection, the motive might have something to do with the Nortel crash, and the opportunity being for the last two victims, the Literary Festival. Where were the other two victims when they were murdered? Sergeant Flowers, do you have the whereabouts of these murders in your notes?"

Sergeant Flowers stood up and flicked through his notes on the unsolved cases. "Yes, Ma'am. James Kidd was working for Murray and Clothier, a finance company in London. He was found dead in his apartment. The previous evening, he had been drinking at The Thirsty Fox. Matt Irons was working in the finance department of Labatt's Brewery in Guelph. He, too, was found dead in his apartment the night after drinking at the Three Stars in downtown Guelph. That's all I have to report, Ma'am."

"Thank you, Sergeant," Susan said, "So all four victims had been drinking before they were murdered. Traces of Flunitrazepam was found in all of their blood toxicology. Our killer had obviously sedated the victims before injecting them."

Constable Ryan put her hand up.

"Yes, Constable Ryan," Susan said trying to mask her impatience.

"Ma'am, assuming that our killer has access to syringes and to potassium chloride, should we presume that he or she works in the medical profession?"

"Constable, we should never assume anything. Although, with that said, I have to say there is a strong possibility that our predator works in the medical profession. He or she could be a pharmacist, a nurse, doctor, or a medical salesman."

Constable Ryan put her hand up again. This time Susan couldn't help the sharpness in her voice.

"Yes, Constable, what is it now?"

"What about veterinarians? Would they have use of potassium chloride?"

"Good questions. All I know is that potassium chloride is used in small doses to reduce blood pressure in humans. Maybe you could find out about the use of it in veterinarian practises. Speaking of which, where is the closest vet?"

Sergeant Flowers answered immediately. "The closest vet is in Zurich, ma'am. There are also vets in Goderich, Clinton, and Seaforth."

"Thank you, Sergeant. Okay, we need to look more closely at our local vets. Here is what I want you to do.

"Constables Elliot and Ryan, I want you to research into the uses of potassium chloride in both humans and animals and I would like you, Constable Ryan to focus on local doctors and nurses and you, Constable Elliot, can focus on the vets and pharmacies. Go back to 2008 and check their backgrounds. Sergeant Flowers, revisit the Nortel collapse and find out which of DFI clients took the biggest fall. And lastly, Sergeant, find the whereabouts of the fifth member of staff working at DFI, Lynda Barnes. She might be the next target on our serial killers list. Go to it team. I feel that we are getting close. Bring back some results."

TWENTY

Rose felt slightly peeved, and then she felt guilty for feeling that way as her sister Kate was having such a good time and boy, did she deserve it. The old adage though of two's company, but three's a crowd, really was true, Rose thought as she watched Kate and her friend, Lynda Forbes, laughing away at some shared joke, leaving Rose to chat to Barry, Lynda's husband, and Tom. It was not that either man was dull company, but she would have liked to have been included in the Lynda and Kate party. Maybe if the other guests had not cried off, then the balance of numbers at the dinner party might have worked better. As it was, the minute that Rose introduced Kate to Lynda, it was as if the two women had instantly bonded and had become soulmates. Oh, well, Rose sighed, Kate needed someone to bring her happiness and who was she to resent that for her heartbroken sister.

Lynda had cooked a delicious dinner of lobster bisque followed by duck in an orange and brandy sauce served on a bed of couscous and lentils. But her piece de la resistance was the amazing Black Forest gateaux she served for dessert. Black cherries soaked in rum nestled on great whirls of chocolate cream piped over the lightest of chocolate sponge cake sandwiched together with more cream. Coffee was served and then port and stilton cheese. By the end of the meal Rose felt that she might burst. Thanking their hosts Lynda and Barry, Rose, Kate, and Tom turned to leave, but before they had even reached the front door Lynda rushed forward and gave Kate a big hug saying, "Please have lunch with me in Goderich tomorrow. I want to check out Samuels. I've heard great things about it. Please say that you'll join me."

Rose turned her head away. She didn't want Lynda to see the hurt in her eyes. She was obviously not included in the invitation and the sense of rejection was quite palpable. Tom, seeing Rose's discomfort, took her hand and spoke. "Right, love, best foot forward, we need to get home to let the dogs out. Thank you both for the lovely evening. Good catching up with you, Barry."

Kate and Lynda made plans for the next day while Rose and Tom started to walk outside into the crisp April evening. Kate ran to catch up with them. She turned to Rose and said, "Your friend is so lovely. I had a wonderful evening. I can't believe that we share the same birth date and everything that Lynda loves, I love too!"

The next morning, after breakfast, Lynda drove up to collect Kate for their day out together. Rose had got over her bout of jealousy and was actually quite looking forward to having the day to herself. She would prepare a lovely dinner for that evening when Paul and Ally would be joining them. In many respects, having Kate out of the way would free Rose up to cook to her hearts delight. Tom was heading out to the Bayview Golf course. Doug had phoned and asked if he would like to join him on their first game of golf of the season.

With the house to herself Rose pulled out the ingredients to make a moussaka. She had purchased a couple of eggplants, zucchini, ground mince, and potatoes. There was always cheese, eggs, and milk in the fridge, plus olive oil, garlic, and tomato paste; standard ingredients that Rose cooked with on a regular basis. She was going to make some fresh artisan bread and a Greek salad to accompany the moussaka and serve hummus and tzatziki with pita bread and olives to start the meal. Any leftovers Paul and Ally could take back with them to London. But what should I do for dessert, Rose thought. Paul's all-time favourite was lemon pudding. Maybe she would make two desserts, a chocolate self saucing pudding and a lemon pudding. Rose set to chopping the onions and garlic for the moussaka; slicing the eggplant, putting that in the oven to roast, and then slicing zucchini and potatoes to boil in water ready to be layered between the cooked ground mince and eggplant. She would conclude the layers with a rich béchamel sauce, finally adding grated cheese on the top.

Rose absolutely loved to cook and Ben and Puff, her beloved dogs, loved her to cook too. She tossed them succulent little morsels as she chopped and baked and often sang to them. Sometimes she put on some music and danced with the dogs, but best of all, Rose always took a break from cooking and took the dogs for a quick walk around the block just to clear the air, she would say. That morning was no exception. Having assembled the moussaka, left the artisan bread dough to rise, and made the two desserts, Rose grabbed the dog's leashes and headed outside.

It was another beautiful April morning with a turquoise sky and just a slight briskness in the air. Rose headed towards Louisa Street and turned right by the old Catholic church which was in the middle of being converted into a beautiful family home. In the distance, on Colina Street, Rose could see the familiar figures of Peggy Grierson and Doctor Glover walking ahead.

It was rather endearing, Rose thought, seeing Dr. Glover accompanying Peggy these days.

They were two lonely widowers seeking out companionship in the twilight of their lives. Although Rose was convinced that Peggy had to be close to eighty, she wasn't one hundred percent sure of her age. When her husband had died, he had been eighty-one and most couples' ages were within a few years of each other. As to Dr Glover, well, he had to be way up into his eighties. He had been widowed since 2009, almost eight years and had only retired a few years ago. People in Bayfield tended to live longer than many other communities, probably because of the relaxed lifestyle most people embraced.

Meanwhile in Goderich, Kate and Lynda had arrived at Samuels ready for an early lunch. Samuels was called a boutique hotel. The whole place had been tastefully renovated and a small restaurant added. Its reputation for fine food had already been established. The two women were shown to a table.

"So, Lynda, why is this place called Samuels?" Kate asked as she nibbled at some crusty bread that had been brought to the table.

"I think that it was named after Samuel Platt. Samuel and a Peter McEwen apparently were drilling for oil on the river flats on the Maitland River. Samuel owned, amongst other things, The Goderich Petroleum Company. After the great black gold rush in Petrolia everybody wanted a slice of the action and drillers popped up all over the place."

Kate interrupted Lynda, "Petrolia? Where on earth is Petrolia? I've never heard of the place before."

Lynda smiled. She adored history and had done a fair amount of research into the history of Southwestern Ontario when Barry and she had first moved to Bayfield.

"Ah, Petrolia, it's about one hour away. Oil was discovered there in the 1860s. By the 1870s, Petrolia was a boom town. It became the biggest tax base in the whole of Canada with millionaires being born overnight. They named the oil, black gold. The town even boasted an opera house and a racetrack. It was the home of Imperial Oil and the founding fathers of Shell and Esso. The whole oil history of that era is fascinating, and I could talk about it for hours, but Samuel Platt never did discover oil when he drilled here in Goderich. Instead, they discovered one of the world's largest deposits of salt. This was around 1866. Last year they celebrated 150 years of salt and had all sorts of festivals. Actually, the history of salt is equally as fascinating as that of oil. All this interesting heritage on our doorsteps. It's really quite amazing."

"So where is the salt mine?" Kate asked while tucking into her lunch of braised steak and onions.

"Oh, it's just down the road by the lake. I tell you what, I'll take you there after we've finished our lunch. We can walk along the boardwalk to Rotary Cove and then maybe have a cup of coffee at The Station."

"That sounds so perfect, Lynda. I'm having such a lovely time. I do, though, feel a bit bad about leaving Rose behind."

"Oh, don't feel bad. Your sister loves nothing better than to bake. She'll be cooking up a storm for your dinner tonight. No, Rose and I can have lunch anytime whereas you're only here for a couple of weeks, so don't feel guilty."

Kate smiled and went back to enjoying her very tasty lunch. Her life wasn't too bad after all, if only she could forget Bob and how he had destroyed her world.

TWENTY-ONE

Back in Bayfield DCI Susan Parker was already at The Lion's Hall a good hour before her team. She had experienced a restless night and had woken up feeling as if she had run a marathon. Now, standing in front of the incident glass she recapped their findings. All four of the victims had died by potassium chloride injections and all four had been employed by DFI from 2005 to 2008. Other than that, there seemed no further link apart from the fact that both Sally Albright and Chris Saul were once married and that both had gone on to become very successful authors.

One thing that had kept re-occurring in Susan's mind during her restless night, was her conversation with Damian Palmer. He had said that Chris Saul had been particularly pushy about trying to get him to invest in Nortel stock which shortly afterwards had crashed. Could the deaths all be connected to someone who might have lost a lot of money through the Nortel debacle? If so, who had invested heavily and lost a fortune, and would that be a strong enough motive for murder?

Susan was still mulling over these possibilities when the team trudged through the door, coffees in hand. She smiled at them and was rewarded by several smiles back. They were a good team, actually, they were an exceptional team and Susan felt almost maternal towards them. She was, after all, old enough to be all of their mothers.

"Okay, everyone, we're getting close to solving these murders. Let's have your reports. Constables Elliot and Brown, what did you find out about potassium chloride?"

Constable Elliot stood up and read from his smartphone, "The majority of potassium chloride produced is used for making fertilizer. It's chemical, metal halide salt is composed of potassium and chloride or KCL. It is inexpensively available and used also for food processing, medicine, and other scientific purposes. Medically, it is used in the treatment of hypokalaemia and associated conditions as an electrolyte replenisher. In cardiac surgery potassium chloride is used to stop the heart beating. High doses can cause cardiac arrest and rapid death. It is used in a third and final lethal injection process for the death sentence execution. In sufficiently high doses it can cause the heart to stop and in death it mimics the appearance of a heart attack. I could find no use of potassium chloride in veterinary practises and only doctors appear to be able to prescribe it. That's all I have, Ma'am."

"Thank you, Constable. Did you procure a list of doctor's prescriptions for potassium chloride in this area?"

"That information is confidential, ma'am. The pharmacies that we spoke to would not divulge that information."

"Okay, fair enough. Right, Sergeant Flowers, who took the biggest fall from the Nortel crash? Which of DFI clients lost the most money?"

The Sergeant coughed to clear his throat and then flicked through his notebook before answering. "There were quite a few, Ma'am, mostly Toronto and London based people. There were a few from this area, several from Goderich and one from Exeter, but there was one significant client who lost over $400,000 and he lives in Bayfield, a Doctor Glover."

There was a shocked silence in the room while the team digested this piece of information. Constable Ryan broke the silence by saying, "Wow, that could certainly be a strong motive for murder. Where does this doctor live?"

"He lives here in Bayfield. I took the liberty to look into his life. He had a practise in the village for thirty years. He also worked for a while at Clinton Hospital helping out in the emergency unit. He retired just after the Nortel crash in 2008 ostensibly to take care of his wife who had a stroke and needed full time care. She died in 2009. He is eighty-five years old and lives alone on Tuyl Street."

Constable Ryan put up her hand, "Isn't he a bit old to be murdering people? And why would he do such a thing?"

Susan paused before answering, "We don't know if he is our serial killer yet, although it certainly sounds as if he could fit the bill. As to the why, Constable Ryan, imagine if you had lost all your life's savings after being advised to invest in shares that were about to go belly up. No, if the doctor is our man, he would certainly have the means, opportunity, and the motive for murder. I suggest that we bring him in for questioning. Sergeant Flowers, any luck in finding the fifth employee of DFI employed during the period of 2005 to 2008?"

Sergeant Flowers stood up again and pulled out his notebook. "Yes, Ma'am, Lynda Barnes married Barry Forbes in 2008. Lynda and Barry live here in Bayfield for six months of the year and then spend the winters in West Palm Springs. They moved to Bayfield from Toronto in 2014. They live on Colina Street."

"Thank you, Sergeant, good work. I would like you to go around to their house. It could be that Lynda's life is in mortal danger. She most certainly needs to be warned. Constable Ryan, you can come with me to apprehend the doctor. We'll all meet back here later this afternoon, say at 4:00 p.m. and see what the doctor has to say. Okay, see you all in a couple of hours."

Constable Ryan stayed behind while the rest of the team filed outside.

"This is where the fun and games begin, Constable," DCI Parker said as she closed her laptop and prepared to leave. "Always be prepared for the unexpected." Susan said as she left the room with Constable Ryan running to catch up.

Rose looked at her watch. It was 3:30 p.m. and still no sign of either Kate or Tom. She had finished her burst of cooking; everything was prepared and ready for their evening meal. Paul had telephoned to say that they would be in Bayfield by 5:30 p.m. and Tom had phoned to say that he would have lunch at the golf club house and probably would not be home before 4:00 p.m.

Rose decided that she would take the dogs for a walk as the sky was still clear and blue and the weather outside looked glorious.

Ben and Puff tugged at their leads and almost pulled Rose over. Just who was taking whom for a walk, Rose thought as she fairly ran along Louisa Street. She had to pull the dogs to a halt when they reached Colina Street. At a more sedate pace they walked along the road until they got to her friend Lynda's house. Rose immediately saw a police cruiser parked out in front of the building. Her heart gave a quick lurch as she felt panic rise in her chest. She walked forward at a quicker pace and marched over to the police officer who was sitting inside the car.

"Umm... officer, are you looking for someone?"

Constable Elliot looked at Rose. He recognized her from previous investigations and calmly replied, "Well, hello, Mrs. Blair. Do you remember me from last year down at the marina? Are these your dogs? They are lovely animals, ma'am."

Rose felt her panic subside a little, but she still wondered what Constable Elliot was doing parked outside her friend's house.

"Are you looking for Lynda Forbes?"

Just as Rose spoke another Constable appeared. He had obviously been at the front door of the house. He nodded at Rose and shook his head to Constable Elliot. "She's not in," he said as he got into the car.

Rose couldn't resist saying, "No, she's in Goderich with my sister Kate."

The two Constables looked at Rose. "So, you know Lynda Forbes?"

Rose answered quickly, "Of course I know her. Lynda is a good friend of mine."

"Well, when you see her can you give her this card with my number? Please tell her it's imperative that she contact the police as soon as possible."

Rose took the card and tucked it into her coat pocket. "But officer, what's wrong? Is Barry okay?"

The one Constable tapped his nose with his finger and said, "It doesn't concern you, Mrs. Blair. Just tell her that it is very important for her to contact us as soon as possible. Good day to you."

Rose felt somewhat slighted. She did not take kindly to being put in her place particularly by police officers who looked like they had barely left school. Pulling the dog's leashes, she headed back towards home determined to get to the bottom of it all before too long. She would phone her friend DCI Susan Parker. Rose knew that she would put her in the picture and tell her exactly what was going on.

TWENTY-TWO

Kate and Lynda were having a great time. After leaving Samuels they drove back over the Maitland River. Lynda pointed out where Tiger Dunlop was buried. She told Kate all about The Canada Company and how they had seduced early settlers over to Canada promising land, schools, and churches when in fact there was nothing but mile upon mile of woodland and swamps. Lynda told Kate all about Baron Van Tuyl and how he had owned most of Bayfield and a large chunk of Goderich at one time way back in the 1840s.

He had to sell most of his land to pay for his property taxes leaving his son, Vincent Van Tuyl to deal with all his debts after he died. Lynda pointed out The Ridge House across the river just down from Tiger Dunlop's tomb, there, she said, was where the Baron had built his hunting lodge.

In its day there had been vineyards planted in terraces down the steep slopes of the ridge overlooking Lake Huron. Kate was fascinated with the history of Huron County and could have listened to Lynda all day long.

They drove to The Square in Goderich and Lynda pointed out

the courthouse and where the tornado had whirled around the square like an out-of-control spinning top destroying everything in its path. That had been in 2011. Kate was amazed that the town looked so pretty. She would never have guessed the extent of the devastation after it had been so badly hit by the tornado. It just went to show the resilience of man over nature and how well the leaders of the community had pulled together to rebuild the infrastructure.

Leaving the town centre, they drove down West Street to the shoreline where the Sifto Salt mine was located. Parking their car in front of The Station restaurant, Lynda and Kate started to walk along the boardwalk towards Rotary Cove. Kate looked at her watch. She was still on Kelowna time, three hours behind Ontario. It was three o'clock. Ally and Paul were not due to arrive in Bayfield before about 5:30. They had plenty of time to kill before heading back home.

Lake Huron was looking particularly beautiful that day with the water sparkling like a myriad of diamonds. It was unusually calm for an April day; no white caps laced the waves. Indeed, the water was as azure blue as blue could be, they could have been in the Mediterranean. Back in Kelowna, Kate thought, Lake Okanagan was lovely, but it definitely looked like a lake with views of the shoreline in all directions. Here, you could be misled into thinking that you were at the seaside; so vast was the stretch of water with no sign of land as far as the eye could see.

A light, cool breeze blew softly. Both women were pleased to be wearing winter jackets as the blue sky and sunshine was very deceptive. It was still only April in Ontario where temperatures, even at their highest, would be under ten degrees. Back in the Okanagan Valley, it could often be up in the high twenties in April.

They continued walking along the boardwalk past a children's play area and a large parking lot on their left. It was mostly rocky beaches alongside the walk, but when they reached Rotary Cove, a lovely expanse of sand lay ahead. There was an off-leash park beyond the other side of the cove, concession stands, and washrooms. Kate could see that at the peak of summer the place would be positively heaving with people and quite a tourist haven.

They walked back to the station restaurant, but found that it was closed. The summer season had not begun yet and quite a few restaurants, particularly in the tourist areas, were not open year-round.

"Should we stop somewhere else for coffee, or should we just go home, Kate?" Lynda asked when they had reached her car.

"Oh, that's up to you, Lynda. I'm easy. It's just so nice not having to go out and feed the chickens and alpacas. We even have a few pigs now to look after and a donkey."

"Who is looking after the livestock while you're here?"

"Oh, I gave Bob an ultimatum. He had to come back from Penticton to look after the farm while I was away, or I promised to get rid of all the animals."

"You wouldn't have, would you?" Lynda said quite alarmed at the prospect of anyone trying to find homes for alpacas and donkeys, let alone pigs and chickens.

"Seriously, well, no, but I'm going to rethink my whole life. It was Bob's dream to have a hobby farm, and whilst I embraced the whole good life thing, I don't think seriously that I can manage the farm by myself. Anyway, I want to travel and have a bit of fun in my old age. Bob will have to decide what to do with all the animals. I'll keep Maisie, our sheep dog, and maybe a couple of the cats, but the other animals, well, Bob will have to find homes for them all."

"Does his, umm... girlfriend have a job? Is she married? Does she have children?"

Kate went very quiet as she thought whether to answer and open up to this newfound friend of hers or not. There was something reassuring and comfortable about Lynda that made Kate feel that she could open up and divulge her innermost secrets.

Lynda's smile turned to a grimace, "Oh, I'm so sorry. I sounded so nosey and pushy just then, please forgive me, I didn't mean to make you feel uncomfortable. Forget that I ever asked you all those personal questions. Okay?"

Kate took Lynda's hand in hers and looked her straight in the eyes.

"Oh, I don't mind telling you about Bob and Natalie. I know that you will keep what I say to yourself. It's just that I still feel very vulnerable talking about it all."

"Look, we'll go home back to my place, and I'll make us both a stiff drink and then, if you want to tell me all about that bastard husband of yours, please feel free to vent forth."

Kate laughed. She had had such a good time with Lynda. Seeing her looking so concerned, she tried to lighten up, "A stiff drink sounds just great. I've got until about 5:30 before I need to be back at Rose and Tom's. Do we pass a LCBO enroot because I would like to buy you a bottle of wine?"

Lynda shook her head, "Absolutely not, my dear friend. Anyway, I've got a wine cellar just full of bottles that Barry keeps buying. With us being away half the year, we are hard pushed to drink what we have in stock let alone Barry constantly buying more. Okay, let's head for home."

With that, the two women left the lake and drove up the hill back towards Highway 21 and Bayfield.

TWENTY-THREE

DCI Parker and Constable Ryan had driven to Dr. Glover's house only to find him not at home. Susan contacted Constable Elliot and asked if he had managed to speak to Lynda Forbes.

"No, ma'am, it appears that she has gone shopping to Goderich."

"How do you know that? Why, is her husband there?" Susan asked.

"Well, Mrs. Blair told me. She said that Ms. Forbes had gone out with her sister for the day. Mrs. Blair was walking the dogs and stopped to ask what we were doing at the Forbes' house."

"Okay, well, thank you, we'll see you shortly at the team meeting."

Susan looked at Constable Ryan and then at her watch. Somehow, she had missed out on eating lunch.

"Do you fancy having something to eat, Constable Ryan?"

Constable Ryan smiled and told Susan that she was starving.

"Do you like Japanese food, Constable?"

"Well...I don't much like raw fish, but I like the Californian sushi and tempura. Oh, and I love edamame beans."

"Right, let's go and check out that new restaurant Drift. We've got about forty minutes before the team meeting."

They pulled up outside the restaurant. It was set quite far back from the road with a spacious patio to the front. In the summer it would be quite jolly with umbrellas and music playing, but now it looked a bit sad. Inside the restaurant was small but friendly, and the aromas coming from the kitchen were quite delicious and made up for the bijoux space. On a chalk board the days special had been marked up. There were three different soups, one a Thai soup, the other, an Irish stew, and the third was a Japanese ramen noodle soup. Also, on special for that day was tonkatsu in a bun served with Japanese fries.

Susan chose the Thai soup and the tonkatsu and Constable Ryan ordered the Raman bowl. Both women chose jasmine tea although preferably they would have ordered a Sapporo beer had they not been on duty.

Susan sighed contentedly. "So, Constable, for now, may I call you Holly?"

"Oh, yes, please do," Holly said, her eyes sparkling with enthusiasm.

"Is this your first murder case?"

"Yes, ma'am. It is and I'm really excited."

"Well, always expect the unexpected. I've been in the police business for over thirty years and no two cases have ever been the same. I suppose that is what I love about the job. Anyhow, I've only ever worked on two serial killer cases before and the last one we never found the killer. It's gone to the cold case files. I think what I'm trying to say is never assume that a case has been sown up until the perpetrator has been convicted, tried, and sentenced. Remember, that our evidence must be absolutely watertight. Many a criminal has gone free by sloppy police work."

Holly nodded. She was in truth quite enthralled to be having lunch with Detective Chief Inspector Parker who was quite the legend back at the headquarters in London. She had been responsible for solving at least five murders in so many years, all based in and around the Bayfield area.

Susan looked at her watch. It was 3:50 p.m.

"Well, officer, we should be getting back to the Lion's Hall. I'll take the bill."

Holly thanked her Chief. She hardly could wait to tell her boyfriend all about her lunch with the infamous DCI Parker.

As they left Drift to return to the Lion's Hall, Susan spotted Peggy Grierson walking along Main Street with her little white fox terrier, Lucy.

She remembered her from a few years ago when there had been a murder at the Town Hall.

Peggy was the Chairperson of the Town Hall committee and had been deeply distressed when the lead singer from the group, The Berries, had been brutally murdered. That case had been a particularly challenging one which, combined with the untimely death of her fiancé, had led to Susan's decision to retire from the police force. She had come out of retirement the following year when she was asked to lead the investigation of the murdered South African couple. Susan had been then promoted to Detective Chief Inspector.

They arrived at The Lion's Hall and DCI Parker separated herself from Holly and walked into the room ahead of the Constable to the waiting team.

TWENTY-FOUR

Lynda and Kate returned just after Constables Elliot and Brown and Rose Blair had departed.

"When will Barry be back?" Kate asked Lynda as they opened the front door and entered the house.

"Oh, probably not before tomorrow. Now, what is your tipple? Gin and tonic, a Manhattan, or just plain wine?"

Kate thought for a minute before answering. "I would just love a gin and tonic. Thanks, wow! This is great."

Lynda disappeared off to the kitchen. Kate could hear the rattle of plates and the opening and closing of the fridge door. Soon she appeared carrying a tray of cheese and crackers, pate, fruit, and two very large gin and tonics.

"Gosh, you're spoiling me," Kate exclaimed as she took the tray from Lynda and put it onto the circular coffee table.

The two women nestled down on the large feather filled cushions of the sofa.

"Cheers," Lynda said as she raised her glass to Kate.

"To friendship," Kate said and sipped her drink.

"You know, I'm not looking forward to telling my daughter about Bob and I," Kate said softly.

"Oh, you'll be surprised. She has probably already guessed. Bob might have already spoken to her, you never know."

"I doubt that he's done anything. Bob always has left the disciplining and confrontational things for me to sort out. I just can't see him telling the kids anything."

"Well, the truth won't hurt as long as you're honest. Ally is old enough to form her own opinion of what's been going on."

Kate sighed, "Yes, I know, but the trouble is Natalie has been a friend of mine and the whole family for years. It's going to be really difficult for the kids to process all of that, I mean, I can still barely believe that it's true myself, let alone the kids."

"When did they start their relationship?" Lynda asked.

"Bob says that he has been in love with her for a couple of years. I was completely unaware of anything going on as was Natalie's husband, Mike."

"How did you actually find out?"

"Well, I didn't. Bob just blurted it out one month ago. He just told me that he didn't love me anymore and that he hadn't for a couple of years and that he was tired of living the lie. I asked him if there was another woman and at first, he wouldn't say who it was, then he said that I'd find out anyway. When he told me that it was Natalie, I didn't believe him at first. I thought that it was some sick joke. When I realized that he was serious I think I was even more shocked by the betrayal of my closest friend then by Bob's unfaithfulness. How could I have not seen the signs?"

Lynda patted Kate's arm and said gently, "Don't, whatever you do, beat yourself up. They obviously were sneaking around behind your back. Have you confronted your friend, Natalie, yet?"

"Oh, yes. The minute that I found out I went right to her house. Mike was away. He's an airline pilot and is often gone for a few days at a time. No, I stormed into her house and demanded to know exactly what was going on between them. I confess to slapping her across her face. She took it all, my ranting and raving, very calmly which made it even worse because I was raring for a fight. When I had calmed down a bit, she just quietly apologized. She said that they had never meant for it to happen, and that Bob and she hated the way they had caused such pain."

"Well, they were consenting adults, of course they could have stopped it from happening." Lynda retorted. "It makes me furious when people say things like that. What a cop out!"

"Yes, I told her that and more. The trouble is, I've lost both the man I love and a best friend, all in one go." Kate could feel her eyes well up. She sniffed loudly and grabbed her purse ready to leave.

"Enough of me and my woes. I really do think that I should go as Rose will be wondering where the heck I've gone."

Kate was just walking towards the front door when there was a loud knock.

"Talk of the devil, I bet that's my sister coming to drag me home. Should I answer it?"

Lynda rose from the sofa and walked towards the door. Kate opened it and was surprised to see an old man standing on the doorstep.

"Oh! Lynda," Kate called over her shoulder, "There's somebody here to see you."

Lynda recognised Dr. Glover immediately. She didn't know him too well but had often seen him walking around the village with Peggy Grierson and her little fox terrier.

"Oh, hello, Doctor, come on in. How can I help you?"

"I just happened to be walking by when I noticed that your garbage bin has been upturned and there is stuff strewn everywhere."

"Oh, it's that racoon again," Lynda said. "I'll come and tidy it up right now."

She turned to the doctor and said, "Please sit a while. I'll be back in a minute and then, maybe, you might like to join us for a drink?"

Kate said that she would help, and the two women went outside leaving the doctor alone in the living room. He had at first been put off by the fact that Lynda was not alone. He had originally planned to make just a social visit initially to check out the layout of the Forbes house. He also wanted to make sure that her husband, Barry, was out of town.

Having had the opportunity given to him on a plate seemed just too good to be true. It would not matter if he was to drug both women however, the big dilemma was should he inject both of them? It was Lynda whom he had waited so long to kill. The last name on the list, the last of the financial team of DFI who had been responsible for ruining his life and ultimately destroying the only love that he had ever known, that of his darling wife, Janet. She had died from cancer, but he knew that her illness had been triggered by the stress of the loss of their lives savings through the Nortel bust.

The Doctor galvanized into action the minute that the two women left the room. How convenient that there were two glasses of drinks already poured out just sitting on the coffee table. He pulled out of his pocket a small vial of Flunitrazepam. Sprinkling liberal amounts of the sleeping drug into each glass he quickly stirred the liquid with his finger to dissolve the powder. Now all he had to do was extend his visit by social chit-chat.

Lynda and Kate returned deep in conversation.

"There, all cleared up," Lynda said turning to the doctor. "Could I offer you a drink, Dr. Glover?"

He quickly said yes and went to sit down on the chair opposite the sofa.

"Kate, let me top up your drink for you. Just a quick one for the road and then I'll let you go," Lynda laughed, not stopping to take no for an answer.

"Oh, alright, you've twisted my arm," Kate said and sat down again opposite the doctor.

"By the way, I'm Kate, Rose Blair's sister," she said extending her hand to him.

"And I'm Dr. Glover. I've been retired for quite some time now, but I practised in the village for over thirty years."

"Oh, then you probably know my sister, Rose?" Kate said as she reached out to take the drink Lynda was offering her.

"Yes, I know Rose Blair. She is very involved in the community."

Lynda sat down and joined them. "Well, cheers everybody," she said and gulped down her gin and tonic. Kate did the same, but the doctor just sipped at his drink.

"Are you sticking around here for a while, Kate?" The doctor asked as he leant forward to take a piece of cheese from the tray on the table.

Kate felt her tongue go numb in her mouth and her eyes suddenly felt incredibly heavy and sleepy. She went to reply to the doctor and realized that she could not articulate the words from her brain to her mouth and even if she could her mouth would not move, and her eyes could barely stay open. She grabbed Lynda and realized that she was leaning sideways, her eyes closed, her head and shoulders slumped against the back of the sofa, and then all Kate could see was darkness...

TWENTY-FIVE

The team were already assembled and waiting for DCI Parker to arrive. Constable's Elliot and Brown looked anxiously at their watches just as their Chief entered the room followed by DC Ryan.

"Yes, Constables, you both look worried. What's the problem?"

Constable Elliot spoke up first, "Well, ma'am, we did go around to Ms. Forbes house, but she wasn't there. We're just a bit worried that she hasn't phoned us as we left a card with our number on it and Mrs. Blair was expecting them back by now. I just have this feeling that something is wrong. Maybe we should return."

"Well, have you tried calling her?" Susan asked trying to hold back her impatience. Sometimes she got tired of having to spoon feed her officers.

"I'll do it right now, ma'am," Constable Elliot said while pulling out his cell phone.

"Right, everyone, anything to report?"

The team all shook their heads. Constable Ryan spoke first. "DCI Parker and I went around to the doctor's house and there was no sign of him. We did see Peggy Grierson walking her dog along Main

Street. Apparently, the doctor and Peggy are friends and are often seen around the village together.

"Thank you," Susan said and continued. "It appears that the doctor is now our prime suspect. We need to apprehend him soon and bring him in for questioning." The phone interrupted Susan just as she was about to continue her speech. "Yes, DCI Parker speaking."

It was Rose Blair sounding decidedly agitated. "Susan, I'm so worried. My sister and Lynda Forbes went shopping hours ago and still haven't returned. It's six o'clock and Kate knew that her daughter and our son were coming here for dinner. I've tried phoning Lynda and there is no answer. I walked the dogs over to her house and they were not there but there was a police cruiser in the driveway. What on earth is going on, do you know?"

"Calm down, Rose and I'll fill you in as much as I can. It appears that your friend Dr. Glover is our prime suspect and your friend, Lynda's life might be in jeopardy. We think that she is on his list of people to kill in some sort of reprisal for his losses. Anyway, it's imperative that we apprehend him quickly. In the meantime, if either Lynda or your sister, Kate makes contact, please warn them to keep away from the good doctor. I'm going to go around to the Forbes house to check things out. Stay calm and leave us to do our job."

Susan put the phone down and thought for a minute. "Team, we're going to park our cars around the corner from Colina Street and go and stake out the Forbes house. Constable Ryan, ride with me. Constable's Elliot and Brown I want you to stake out the rear of the property, Sergeant Flowers, I want you around the front. If needs be, we'll break the door down."

The team left quickly with Susan in the lead.

TWENTY-SIX

Rose put the phone down and paced the floor. Tom had come in but then had gone out again to help fix Doug's television. He had not been at all concerned when Rose had expressed her worries about Kate and Lynda's whereabouts. Tom just knew how women liked to shop and, in his mind, he visualized the women just getting carried away and forgetting about the time.

Rose decided that she would walk the dogs once more around the block. They could never get enough walks and it would do her good to get some fresh air. That way she could also check to see if Lynda's car was in the driveway although why she was not answering her phone was a mystery. Lynda was normally very good at communicating, particularly by phone.

Puff and Ben frolicked in the hallway while Rose put on her jacket and found their leashes. Soon they were trotting down Louisa Street and turning onto Colina. Five minutes later Rose found herself at the back of Lynda's house. She could see a light on in the main room. As she rounded the corner, she immediately noticed that the curtains of the living room were wide open and the light full on. She could see the figure of a man silhouetted in the light. So, they were in,

Rose thought as she rounded the corner and saw Lynda's car parked in the driveway. She marched up to the front door and was about to knock when she noticed that the door was slightly open. "Lynda, Kate, are you home?" Rose called out feeling a bit uncomfortable entering her friend's house on her own. Yet she had definitely seen someone in the living room.

Rose let go of the dog's leashes and they went pounding into the living room ahead of her.

"Puff, Ben, wait for me," Rose cried and then her voice died out as she viewed the tableaux before her. There, slumped on the sofa, was her sister and Lynda. Oh, no, I'm too late, they're dead, Rose thought. Ben and Puff jumped up and down in a frenzy barking at the man who, to Rose's amazement, was none other than Dr. Glover. He appeared to be advancing upon the two women on the sofa. In his hand he held a syringe. Rose suddenly understood. Dr. Glover was indeed the serial killer. Her friend Susan had said as much on the phone, but she foolishly had not believed her. How could the good doctor be the murderer? He was Peggy Grierson's friend and a long-standing resident of Bayfield. But sure enough he was intent on using the syringe.

"Ben, Puff, stop barking," Rose shouted, and Dr. Glover turned around at the sound of Rose's voice. His eyes pierced into hers almost pleadingly.

"Dr. Glover, put that syringe down. Please give it to me," Rose said her voice shaking as she stepped forward, her arm outstretched to receive the syringe.

"Rose Blair, you cannot stop me now. This is my destiny." His voice rose to a high pitch as he shrieked out, "She must die, the last one must die."

As he lunged forward, Ben bit one of his ankles and Puff ran circles and circles around him, both dogs barking like crazy. Dr. Glover flayed his arms in the air and attempted to kick the dogs. Rose dove at him and before she knew what was happening the two of them were on the floor in a pile of arms and legs and the dogs were still barking and nipping at the doctor who struggled to get up. Rose saw the syringe still clasped in his hand. She stretched out to grab it from him and then, just as she thought that she had succeeded, she felt an almighty kick to her head. Pain shot through, everything started spinning, and then there was only darkness...

TWENTY-SEVEN

Constable Ryan was first on the scene. As soon as DCI Parker had pulled up her car in front of the Forbes house, Holly was out of the car and running. The front door was open. As she ran into the living room, she could hear dogs barking. At first, she thought that the three women were all dead. Two lay slumped on the sofa, a third stretched out on the floor. The old man, Dr. Glover, was surrounded by the dogs who were nipping at his ankles and growling menacingly. Susan Parker ran in behind Holly and called the dogs off.

DCI Parker drew out her gun and shouted. "Dr. Glover, you are under arrest!"

The doctor looked over at Susan defiantly and then, without any warning, and without a word, he injected the syringe into his own neck. Both DCI Parker and Constable Ryan looked on hopelessly. There was nothing they could do.

He had chosen to take his own life instead of being arrested.

"Quick, call for an ambulance," Susan shouted as she glanced at Rose who lay comatose on the floor. Dr. Glover had crumpled like a sack of potatoes and after a few convulsions his eyes glazed over and in minutes he was dead.

Susan rushed over to Rose who lay inert. She felt her pulse. It was very slow, and her breathing was shallow. As for Kate and Lynda, they were obviously in a deep sleep. Every now and then Kate let out a snuffled snore and Lynda's mouth moved as if she was talking, yet both women were totally oblivious to the macabre scene before them.

Susan looked at her friend again, concern etched into her face. Hurry up paramedics, she thought, as again she phoned in for help. Then, finally, Susan heard the siren getting louder and louder as it neared the Forbes' house. Soon the living room was awash with paramedics. Kate and Lynda were strapped onto a stretcher and taken to the first ambulance. The dead doctor was zipped up into a body bag and removed to another vehicle while the paramedics worked on Rose.

A neck brace was gently put around her neck and an oxygen mask attached to her face. She was cautiously lifted onto another stretcher still unconscious. As Rose was hoisted into the air, Susan noticed the side of her head. There was blood oozing out of a deep gash and her hair was all matted and caked with congealing blood. Oh my gosh, Susan thought, let this not be serious. She reached for her cell phone and called Tom.

Tom had helped Doug to get his new television, a smart t.v., programmed. Doug was a good golf player, but not very practical when it came to technical matters. He had purchased a 60-inch LED Sony Smart TV, and it remained in its packaging for two whole weeks before he had enlisted Tom's help.

After they had the television up and running, the two men enjoyed a beer together until Tom looked at his watch and realized the time. It was almost six o'clock and Rose would be wondering where the heck he had got to. Rushing off from Doug's house he had driven down Main Street and turned right onto Catherine.

As he reached the Forbes' house, he was immediately faced with what looked like a war zone. Three ambulances, all with their lights flashing, and four OPP cruisers flanked the outside of the house. Tom slowed down and when he saw DCI Susan Parker appear at the doorway with another young female officer, he clicked down his window and called out,

"What's going on here, Susan?"

Susan looked surprised to see Tom. "I've just been trying to reach you on the phone. Please pull over here and let me explain what's happened."

Tom could hear the seriousness in her voice and immediately felt apprehensive. He pulled over and stopped the engine. Just as he got out of the car, two stretchers were being wheeled out of the Forbes house. He immediately recognized both Lynda and Kate.

"What the hell is going on here?" Tom demanded, panic reaching up his throat.

"Stay calm. I'll explain, but first I need you to know that Rose has been injured."

Before Susan could finish what she was about to say, Tom had pushed past her and ran into the living room where Rose was still lying on the stretcher, her face as white as marble with her neck supported by a brace.

"Oh, my God. Rose, my darling." Tom exclaimed.

The paramedics had to stop Tom from embracing his wife. "Please do not move her, sir," one of the paramedics said. "She's sustained a serious injury to her head. We won't know how bad it is until she has had a scan."

Tom could see blood matted in her hair. He suddenly felt light-headed and stumbled forward.

"Quick, sit down, mate." The other paramedic said to Tom, "you're in shock. Put your head down and take a deep breath."

Tom indeed felt faint. He had a distinct sense of unreality. This surely could not be happening to him. What exactly had happened and why?

Susan Parker came and sat down next to Tom on the sofa. She took his hand in hers and said gently,

"Tom, she's going to be alright you know. Look, she saved Lynda and Kate's lives. She's a hero."

Before she could say anything else they were interrupted by the paramedics w, andishing to lift the stretcher into the ambulance. Tom got up and walked beside them and asked if he could ride with them in the ambulance.

"Best you not, sir. Follow us in your own vehicle." one of the paramedics said.

Tom got into his car still feeling as if he was an onlooker watching a play or certainly something that wasn't really happening, like a reality show. The red lights on the ambulance started to flash, and they were off at a great speed heading towards Clinton and the emergency wing.

On the way there, Tom kept replaying in his head the ghastly scene that he had witnessed in the Forbes living room. Susan still hadn't explained what exactly had taken place. He would have to wait to hear the full story, but right now all he could focus on was Rose, his darling Rose.

An hour later Tom was still pacing up and down in the waiting room of Clinton Hospital. His cell phone rang. It was Paul.

"Dad, where are you and Mom? Ally and I have been waiting here for ages. The dinner was in the oven which fortunately wasn't burnt, but where are the dogs? What's happening?"

At the mention of the dogs Tom audibly groaned. In his anxiety for Rose, he had completely overlooked them.

"Paul, your mother is in hospital. I don't even know the whole story yet, but I might be here a long time."

"What about Aunt Kate? Where is she? Dad, what on earth is going on?"

"Look, son, all I can say is your mom is in a serious condition." Tom felt his voice thicken and his eyes well up. He took a gulp of air and then continued.

"The best thing you can do is to eat the dinner your mother prepared, she wouldn't want it wasted, and then come over here. I'm at the Clinton Hospital in the emergency ward."

Just then the doctor appeared and beckoned Tom to follow him.

"You're Mr. Blair I presume? I'm Dr. Powell." He led Tom into a small office and pulled out an envelope containing an x-ray which he clipped to a light box mounted on the wall.

"This is your wife's skull. Note this mass here." The doctor, using a pen, pointed to what looked like a cloudy area on the screen. "This is a large pool of blood here, caused from the kick to her head. It's known as epidural hematoma, intracranial bleeding. We may have to transfer her to London for surgery if the blood doesn't stop pooling. There is a procedure called endovascular coiling which can be done, but we will just have to wait and see if the internal swelling goes down first before we make that decision."

"Is Rose conscious?" Tom asked anxiously.

"No. She is still in a coma and that is the best thing for her at the moment. She was badly concussed by the blow to her head. I have to warn you that we are moving her to the intensive care unit."

Tom sighed audibly and then he remembered Kate and Lynda. "What about the two women who were brought in at the same time as my wife?" Tom asked hesitatingly.

The doctor sighed and shrugged his shoulders.

"Oh, they're still asleep, totally out of it. They were drugged with a strong dose of Flunitrazepam, commonly known as Rohypnol, the rape drug."

Tom must have looked alarmed because the doctor hastily added, "No, they've not been raped at all. They'll probably sleep for twenty hours or so and wake up with absolutely no memory of the event."

"Oh, well at least that's good news," Tom said and meant it. He couldn't have dealt with facing Ally, Kate's daughter if it had been more serious. He was barely holding it together himself with Rose being so critical.

"You know something, Mr. Blair, you should go home and get some rest. The staff will call you if there are any changes to your wife's condition."

Tom nodded. The last thing in the world he could do right now was sleep. There was, however, Paul and the girls to consider. He would go home and make a few phone calls.

As it happened, a very panicked Paul and Ally pulled up into the car park just as Tom was walking out to his car.

"Dad, Dad, how is Mom?" Paul cried out.

Followed by a worried Ally who said, "And what about my mother, is she okay?"

"Hold your horses, you two." Tom said. "Look, Ally, your mother is fine. She was drugged and is sleeping it off right now. Paul, Mom is in a coma and is in the intensive care unit. They have told me to go home. They'll call if there are any changes."

Paul's face creased up with worry. "Will she be alright?"

"Yes, son, she's in good hands." Tom said, although he wasn't quite sure himself, sounding more confident than he actually felt. The doctors were great, but haemorrhaging of the brain sounded awful and didn't bear thinking about. With a deep sigh, he said, "Look, we'll all go home now and get some rest. I need to telephone your sisters."

Twenty minutes later Tom, Paul, and Ally were back home. The house seemed so quiet without the dogs. Quite where the dogs were Tom couldn't fathom, but he had other more pressing things on his mind. There was a message on the telephone. It was Susan Parker.

"Tom, I've got Puff and Ben here. Give me a call as soon as you get in and I'll bring them over."

At least that was one mystery solved. Tom still hadn't been told exactly what had happened to Rose inside the Forbes house. Hopefully Susan would be able to fill him in with the details, well, as much as she might know herself, he thought.

Susan had herself been over to Clinton Hospital to check up on Rose and the other women, Kate and Lynda. She was very concerned to hear that Rose had been transferred to the ICU and was not allowed visitors other than family members. She had managed to collar a doctor who had reluctantly told her that Rose had sustained severe cranial haemorrhaging and that the condition was very serious. As far as Lynda and Kate were concerned, they would sleep like babies until the next day and should wake up feeling rested and oblivious to the ordeal. They would certainly be able to make a police statement, but just how much they would remember was iffy. But as to her friend Rose, Susan shook her head. What would Tom do without her if she didn't pull through?

TWENTY-EIGHT

When Tom arrived home Paul and Ally suggested that they all have a stiff drink. Tom looked exhausted and was very agitated.

"Dad, we need to let Jessica and Annie know about mom. Do you want me to call them?"

Tom nodded. He couldn't face talking to anyone yet. The image of his wife's white face and her blood matted head kept flashing through his mind. What if she didn't make it through the night? Oh God, I should be there by her side, Tom thought.

"Look, Paul, I can't stay here. I must go back to the hospital. I need to be with your mother."

Paul could see and feel his father's pain. "Go then. I'll make the calls and Ally and I will stay and look after things here. Don't you worry, just go and give Mom a kiss from me."

Tom grabbed his coat and rushed out of the house. Rose needed him now more than ever. He would move heaven and earth to see her smile again.

Meanwhile Susan had called her team in for one last meeting. She knew that they would all be anxious to hear about Rose, but unfortunately there was little that she could report on that regard. Susan stood up and addressed her team.

"Good evening everyone. I won't keep you long as we've all had an arduous day. Firstly, I need to confirm that Dr. Glover did indeed kill himself with a lethal injection of potassium chloride. By the looks of things, Rose Blair tried to stop him from injecting the two women, Kate and Lynda who were drugged with a big dose of Rohypnol. In trying to avert the murders, she was kicked in the head and has suffered massive cranial bleeding. Rose is in a coma in the ICU at Clinton Hospital."

Susan looked visibly shaken by her friend, Rose's injuries. It crossed her mind whether this would mean a conflict of interest as she was so close to one of the victims, but she wasn't going to be the one to make that call. She continued briefing her team with a slightly shaky voice.

"It is pretty conclusive that Dr. Glover murdered Chris Saul and Sally Albright. He probably killed Matt Irons and James too. The fact that all four worked for DFI in Toronto during the same time as the Nortel collapse and that Lynda Forbes was also one of the same team, points to a strong motive for murder. He had the means alright, potassium chloride would be readily available to any medical practitioner, and he had the opportunity when the Literary Festival presented Chris and Sally as their guest speakers. Dr. Glover must have tracked Lynda Forbes down. The fact that she was away for six months of the year ran in her favour. He must have been just waiting for her return. So, there we have it, means, motive, and opportunity. The three mainstays of any murder enquiry."

Susan looked at her watch. It was 9:15 p.m., time to wrap up the meeting and send her team home. She hadn't yet heard from Tom. Puff and Ben were still in her car and probably getting rather cold. Susan suddenly felt drained of energy. She needed to get home and have an early night, but she was feeling too anxious about Rose to sleep. She shook her head and continued her debriefing with the team who also looked tired and in need of a well-earned rest.

"Okay, everyone, a job well done. We'll have a complete debriefing session on Friday after all the reports have been filed. I will personally take the statements from the two women tomorrow when they are a wake. Any final questions?"

Constable Ryan put her hand up. "Yes, ma'am. in a case when the perp kills himself does the Crown still have to prosecute?"

"Good question, Constable. The simple answer is in a clear-cut case like this where there was no evidence of anyone aiding or abetting Dr. Glover, then the case is declared closed. Of course, I have to write up an extensive report and forensics has to prove beyond a reasonable doubt that he took his own life, but those are all just formalities. Normally a serial killer on trial, particularly one with a history of killing over a period of a five-year span, the trial could last sometimes years and even then, with no guarantee of a conviction. These days there is absolutely no room for sloppy police work. Many a murderer has been acquitted on technicalities alone, so we have to be particularly relieved that our case had ended with a closure. Right, everyone, once again thank you. It has been a pleasure working with you all again and a real pleasure having you, Constable Ryan, on our team."

Holly smiled from ear to ear and her face turned bright red with embarrassment. Her first murder case with the legendary DCI Parker and here she was being welcomed warmly by the woman herself. It somehow made all the hard work and the hassle of working in a predominantly male profession, much more worthwhile. Maybe being a police officer might not be too bad after all, she thought as she said her goodbyes to DCI Parker. This thought was instantly followed by a sense of regret, maybe this might be the only murder case that she gets to investigate under the leadership of DCI Parker.

With the team all gone, Susan was left in the incident room alone. There was always a sense of loss, of anti-climax, and deflation after any conclusion of an investigation. This time she felt it even more acutely. Maybe it was because the murderer had taken his own life or maybe it was because she was deeply worried about her friend Rose Blair, but whatever, Susan Parker suddenly felt deeply depressed.

"I should have stayed retired," she said aloud to the empty walls of The Lion's Hall.

TWENTY-NINE

Tom was just reversing out of his driveway when Susan pulled up outside his house. She jumped out of her car and opened the back door to let two most anxious and hungry dogs out. Puff and Ben bounded over to where Tom had stopped and was getting out of his car.

"Tom, I'm so sorry, I meant to drop the dogs off sooner, but my team meeting took priority. How is Rose?"

Tom grabbed Puff and Ben by their collars and pulled them over to the front door of his house. He opened the door and let the dogs run excitedly inside. Paul and Ally would take care of them now. He turned and walked over to where Susan stood. The man looked exhausted and haggard, his face was strained and his skin pale. Lines of worry were etched into his every pore. Poor, poor, Tom, Susan thought as she extended her arms to receive him in an embrace.

Tom welcomed Susan's hug and before he could stop himself, he felt great tears rolling down his cheeks and his body started to shake as he desperately attempted to contain the deep sob trying to escape from his throat. Susan felt Tom's shaking body and held him even tighter.

"Don't you worry Tom. Rose will pull through. She's stronger than she looks."

Tom sniffed loudly and said with a deeply choked up voice, "She's in the intensive care unit. They're trying to stabilize the cranial bleeding, but it doesn't look good. Oh my God, Susan, I can't lose her now."

"Tom, try to stop being so negative. You go back to the hospital and talk to Rose. She may be in a coma, but she will still hear you. Tell her how much you love her and don't let her hear any of that negativity." Susan said biting her lips. Sometimes one had to be cruel to be kind and right now Tom couldn't afford to fall about at the seams. Rose needed him to be strong now more than ever.

Tom pulled himself together, straightened his back, and prepared to get back in the car.

"Thank you, Susan. I was actually on my way back to the hospital. You're quite right. Rose does need me, and I need her."

With that he got back into the car and drove off towards Clinton. Susan sighed. Tom and Rose had been married for forty-five years and were still very much in love. Would she herself ever find the love of her life? So far, she had one failed marriage, which had only lasted all of four years, one almost marriage to Henri, and a couple of extramarital affairs. Then there were the countless online dating liaisons, most of which had been nothing more than a farce. Her relationship with Peter Joyce the photographer was okay, but Susan didn't feel as if he was the love of her life. When will I find love, she thought for the hundredth time as she drove back to her condo at Harbour Court which she knew would be dark and decidedly unwelcoming.

THIRTY

When Anne heard about her mother, she was just putting Oliver to bed. He had been bathed and had his bedtime story, but now he was being restless and crying for his daddy. It had been one of those long days that seemed to go on forever.

Anne was a Professor at Dalhousie University as was her husband, Allan. They had moved to Halifax from Toronto three years ago and had fallen in love with Nova Scotia. Anne, however, had just recently found out that she was expecting their second child. She hadn't told anyone yet, preferring to wait until the first trimester was over.

Besides, being an older mother there could be complications. At thirty-eight, the doctors had warned her of the increased risk of Down Syndrome, but she had had the test and that was okay. Now her three months were up, and it was time to tell everyone that she was pregnant.

Anne, had in fact been about to call her parents to tell them their news when Paul had telephoned her.

"Anne, Mom's in the intensive care unit of Clinton Hospital. She was kicked in the head and has suffered bleeding to the brain."

Anne interrupted her brother, "Hey, Paul, hold on a minute, what do you mean kicked in the head? Who would kick Mom in the head?"

"Sis, it's complicated. Mom was trying to stop someone from injecting a lethal dose of potassium chloride into her friend Lynda and Aunt Kate. It's a long story, but the upshot is that in the struggle mom got kicked in her head and it's caused internal bleeding."

"Is she going to be alright?" Anne said her voice rising with alarm.

"We don't honestly know. She's in a coma and Dad's there by her side as we speak."

"I think that I should fly out. Look, if I can get a flight I'll try to get to London by tomorrow and maybe you could pick me up from the airport?"

"I don't think you should come just yet. What will you do with Oliver? You know, there is nothing anyone can do. Mom is in a coma, and she may stay that way for weeks. Give it a few days and see what happens, hey."

"Oh, Paul, I wanted to tell Mom and Dad that we're expecting another baby." Anne could feel her eyes well up and her voice quiver.

"That's great news! Look, you can still tell Mom and Dad your news. Why don't you phone Dad tomorrow and maybe he can get you to tell Mom yourself on the phone. She might be in a coma, but I'm sure that she can hear what people are saying."

"You're right. I'll delay flying over for a couple of days and yes, I'll phone Dad tomorrow, but you promise to let me know if there are any changes to mom's condition, good or bad." Anne paused and then continued, "Since when, bro, have you got to be so sensible?"

"Umm... probably since I've become a teacher. All those twenty-year-olds really make me feel old."

"Are you still seeing that student, what was her name, Matty, Marty, or something like that?"

Paul had been dating a Spanish girl, an ESL student from Fanshawe College. Jessica, his older sister had not approved one single bit and had let him know in no uncertain way that she considered him a prize jerk. Jessica had been particularly close to Atsuko, his ex-wife, although technically they were still married. On reflection, Paul mused, he had been on the rebound from his separation from Atsuko and the relationship with Marty had not lasted long at all, barely one semester.

He sighed and answered his sister, "No, Marty and I parted ways ages ago. I'm not seeing anyone right now. I might be flying out to Japan to see Atsuko again."

"Oh, Paul, does that mean you two might be getting back together?"

Paul thought about it for a minute before answering his sister. The trouble was he wasn't even sure of his own feelings yet and wasn't quite sure what Atsuko felt either. They had spoken on the phone for hours, had even Facetimed together, and it had felt so good just chatting away like old times.

"I don't know, I really don't know. Atsuko's dad died, and she's taken it badly. She also split up with her boyfriend and I think that she's feeling really lonely and very depressed. I'm thinking of spending a couple of weeks in Japan and will take it from there."

"Well, Paul, I hope that you can work it out together. Atsuko is lovely and you know the whole family would welcome her back anytime."

"Thank you, Anne. I'm going with an open mind. We'll just have to see how things go." Paul could hear Oliver, his little nephew's voice in the background calling for his mom.

"Paul, I have to go, Oliver's calling. I'll phone Dad tomorrow. Love you."

Paul held the phone in his hand one minute longer. He missed his sister. They had always been close, not like his sister Jessica, who permanently thought that his parents spoilt him and that he was their golden boy. He had lived in London now for almost a year and she had never invited him over for dinner or anything during that time. Despite that, he loved her all the same. His family meant the world to him, and Abby and Ella were just the best nieces in the whole wide world.

He tapped in Jessica's number. She answered almost right away.

"Oh, hi Paul. What's up?"

Paul gave his sister the whole story as much as he knew himself. He waited for her reaction.

"Oh my God. Is Mom going to be alright?"

He could hear the worry in her voice. Jessica wasn't as sensitive as Anne and certainly was not prone to melodrama. He answered her levelly, "We don't know, Jess. There is bleeding in the brain, and you know how tricky that can be, I mean anything to do with the head is problematic. She's in a deep coma and there's nothing anyone can do but wait."

"I should come over. I can't bear to think of poor Dad coping on his own. Oh my God, it's awful."

"Well, you should come over tomorrow, but don't bring Abby and Ella. They wouldn't be allowed to visit their grandma anyway and it would frighten them seeing Mom in a coma. See if you can come here after you've dropped the girls off at school. Ally and I have to get back to London so Dad will be pleased to have some company. If there are any changes in Mom's condition you must phone both Anne and I and we'll come as soon as we can."

"Right, I'll do that, and I'll stay and make Dad some dinner before I go back in time for the girls to be picked up from school. I'm so glad that you were in Bayfield for Dad, Paul."

"Yes, well, I do feel inadequate. All I can do is take the dogs for a walk and make telephone calls. The phone hasn't stopped ringing since people have found out that Mom is in hospital."

"Okay, I must go now. See you, Paul," Jessica said and put the phone down realizing that she felt quite faint with worry.

THIRTY-ONE

Susan had shaken herself out of her low spirits and had decided that she might as well spend the rest of the evening writing up her final summary of the murder at The Little Inn. The team had all handed in their reports and it was up to her as team leader to read and paraphrase them into one clear brief.

Susan started to plough her way through each officer's statements. One hour later she was going googly eyed with reading and typing when she suddenly stopped mid-sentence and re-read what was in front of her.

It was Sergeant Flowers' report on the two cold case murders of James Kidd and Matt Irons. The evidence was conclusive that the killer had the same profile as Dr. Glover. The use of potassium chloride as a lethal injection was the main link, but the fact that James and Matt were also past employees of DFI and hence were on the doctor's hit list, had sealed the connection positively.

There was, however, just something about the case that niggled Susan. She re-read the case histories again until it came to the forensic report and the DNA testing. Although the results of Dr.

Glover's DNA were unknown, it had been standard procedure in the other victims to take samples for DNA testing. Traces of the murderer had been found on both victims and the DNA had been noted in the report Susan was reading.

What had caused Susan to pause and gasp was the fact that the gender marker on the DNA samplings for both Matt and James showed that the murderer must have been female. Oh my gosh, Susan thought, we made the grand assumption that Dr. Glover had killed all four victims when in fact he couldn't have killed the two cold cases. Yet everything else about the profiles tied in with the case histories. So, if Dr Glover was not the murderer, then who was the perpetrator?

Susan rubbed her eyes and read up the investigation notes on both Matt Irons and James Kidd. She compared the DNA results of both cases and at last could verify that whoever had killed James had also killed Matt as the traces of DNA found on both bodies were the same.

"So, what do we know about these men?" Susan said out aloud. She began to itemize the known facts. Firstly, they both worked for DFI at the same time as Sally Albright and Chris Saul and not forgetting Lynda Barnes. They therefore would all have been on Dr. Glover's list, yet he had only managed to kill two of the five people.

The opportunity had been handed to him on a plate when both Sally and Chris had been invited to the Bayfield Literary Festival. Lynda Forbes was saved from certain death by Rose Blair's intervention. The common factor was that three out of the five victims happened to be in Bayfield, the other two were murdered in different locations. Did that mean that Dr. Glover had an accomplice? Susan thought, a female accomplice, and if so, who could she be?

Without doubt she would have to call the team back in and re-open the case. If her theories made any sense, then there could well be a killer still at large.

Susan made her phone calls and looked at her watch. It was only 8:30 p.m., hopefully the team could be assembled within the hour which would give her a little time to grab something to eat before going out.

THIRTY-TWO

Tom had been at Rose's bedside for a solid three hours and he was beginning to feel in need of a cup of coffee or something to keep him going. He would pop over to the Tim Horton's on Highway 8 and grab a sandwich and coffee. Kissing Rose gently he told her where he was going. Tom wasn't sure if she could hear him or not, but he had read that coma patients often felt reassured by touch and background noise. "I love you, darling. I'll be back in twenty minutes, so don't go away, love." Tom said before leaving the room.

The hospital was dead quiet. Tom wondered if Kate and Lynda had woken up yet. Probably not, he thought, he would check up on them in the morning if he could find where they were bedded. The intensive care ward was separate from all other wards and Tom always felt confused and disoriented in hospitals, they all seemed like rabbit warrens to him.

Twenty minutes later Tom was just pulling into the hospital car park when he noticed a car that he recognized from Bayfield. He wracked his memory trying to remember who drove the silver Lexus and then it came to him. The car belonged to Peggy Grierson.

Tom walked back to the I.C, ward and sat down on the same chair he had vacated a little while ago. Maybe Peggy had come to visit Rose, he thought as he looked down upon his wife's face. Was it his imagination or had Rose's hand just moved from where he had left it? Her face still looked the same, but maybe, just maybe her eyelids were fluttering just a little bit. Tom had to stop himself from imagining too much, he knew most of it was just wishful thinking. Taking Rose's hand in his he squeezed it, saying, "I'm back, love, it's just you and me again."

THIRTY-THREE

Meanwhile, the Serious Crimes team had returned to The Lion's Hall all with questioning looks etched on their faces. Susan felt bad as just a few hours ago they had been celebrating the wrap up of the case and now she had to tell them that it was still open.

"Good, evening, everyone. So, sorry to drag you all back here again at this time of night, but I'm afraid that we have some loose ends to tie up. It appears that the good doctor must have had an accomplice, a female one at that. Let me explain..."

Ten minutes later Susan opened up the room for discussion. Constable Ryan put her hand up.

"Yes, Constable," Susan said.

"Well, from what I remember from my notes the doctor was widowed six years ago so his wife cannot have been his accomplice as the two cold cases took place after her death. But Ma'am, what about the lady we've seen him with, you know, the one with the little dog? She was with him at the literary festival and was interviewed at The Little Inn as a witness to the fight between Damian Palmer and Chris Saul."

Constable Ryan paused to flick through her notes. "Here we are, Ma'am. Her name is Peggy Grierson. I've got her address and everything down in my notes."

Susan nodded, "Right, maybe you two could go and pay Mrs. Grierson a little visit but wait until the morning. It's too late to be paying little old ladies visits right now. We don't want to frighten her off. Now, anymore thoughts?"

Sergeant Flowers put his hand up. "Well, Melissa Manson and Pippa Hargreaves both were connected to the deceased authors and Pippa has a medical background."

Susan wrote the women's names on the glass incident board.

"Now, we need to see if any of these women have any connection to Dr. Glover." She pointed to Peggy Grierson's name and continued, "We know that Peggy and Dr. Glover were friends, good friends, but what about Melissa and Pippa? We need to delve into their pasts to see if either of them knew the doctor. Right, team, we have to act fast. If this accomplice learns that the doctor is dead and was unsuccessful in his quest to kill Lynda Forbes, who knows what she might do. My intuition tells me that she will want to complete his plan to eliminate the team of DFI employees responsible for the doctor's huge financial loss. For someone to kill for someone else that tells me that the person has to be very close to our deceased doctor, so here's what we're going to do. Constable Brown and Elliott you already have your briefing, but don't forget to go gently with Peggy. She may not know that the doctor is dead. Sergeant Flowers, I want you to search Dr. Glover's house and see if you can find any connections to Peggy, Melissa, or Pippa. Look for letters, photos, check his computer and cell phone, and get the tech guys in on that."

"Constable Ryan, you and I are going to pay both Melissa and Pippa a visit. They may not know yet about Dr. Glover's death and I want our visit to be a surprise. Constable, look up their addresses and be prepared to leave as soon as possible."

Constable Ryan looked perplexed, "But, ma'am, it will take us at least three hours to get to Toronto and that will mean it will be way past midnight when we get there."

Susan thought for a minute. "Yes, you're quite right. I'll contact the Toronto Police and ask them to bring the women in for questioning. That way we get to travel up early tomorrow morning and we'll be ready to interview them. So, are there any more questions?"

There was silence in the room, even Constable Ryan seemed to have dried up.

Susan continued. "Can you think of any more women who could have cared enough about Dr. Glover to risk everything? He had no children, his wife died before our cold case murders, and he had no known relatives as far as we can see. Is there anyone else we've overlooked?"

Constable Ryan put her hand up. "Well, it's far fetched I know, but what about the owner of The Little Inn, Joanne? She lived in Toronto before moving to Bayfield and she seemed very calm over the deaths at The Little Inn. I don't know, it was just a thought."

Susan did think that it sounded somewhat far fetched, but at least the young Constable was thinking outside the box.

"It could be a possibility and we cannot rule out any ideas. Maybe you can look into her past and see if you can find any connection to our doctor. Okay, go to it everyone. We'll meet back here tomorrow afternoon when we get back from Toronto."

The team departed leaving Susan in complete silence. She felt distinctly agitated and frustrated as much with herself as to anyone else. How could they have missed the fact that the two cold case murders were undeniably not the work of Dr. Glover?

The DNA markers were undeniably gender specific and, in this case, definitely female. In their haste to wrap up the case, DNA sampling had not even been matched to either that of Dr. Glover or the two cold cases. They would have to take samples of the doctor's DNA to definitively clarify that he, indeed, had murdered Chris Saul and Sally Albright. Sloppy police work, Susan thought, and I should know better. She reached for her cell phone and called the forensics doctor in Goderich.

"Ian Green speaking."

"Hi Ian," Susan said. "I'm so sorry to call you this late, but I just wanted to ask you a question about our murders in Bayfield. Firstly, did you take DNA swabs from both Chris Saul and Sally Albright?"

Ian replied, "Yes, we always take swabs for DNA testing. It's standard procedure, all part of a set protocol that we have to follow. Why do you ask?"

"And have you taken DNA swabs from Dr. Glover's body, the suicide case brought in late this afternoon?"

"Yes, that was done when the body was admitted to the mortuary. I haven't yet conducted a full and thorough postmortem. I believe he's on the block first thing tomorrow morning."

"Is there anyway that you can expedite the results of the DNA sampling from all three victims? It's imperative that we get those results and fast."

"Well, all our lab work is outsourced, but I'll call the laboratory and see if they can fast track our tests. It will all depend on the back log. But why the rush? Surely you have your killer. I thought that it was the doctor? He certainly killed himself with a syringe full of potassium chloride which matches the same method used on both Chris Saul and Sally Albright."

Susan let out a deep sigh. Should she confide in Dr. Green or not? He was after all seconded to the police as a forensic pathologist and as such not allowed to discuss cases in public. Besides, she quite liked the man in a quirky sort of way. He reminded her of Bill Nye the Science Guy on television.

"The problem is we think that the doctor had an accomplice, maybe a female nurse or at least someone with a medical background. We made the wrong assumption that the doctor was responsible for the murdering of two other men killed several years ago. The method of killing was the same lethal injection. Anyway, DNA results taken at the scene of the murders proves that the assailant must have been female. Now we are wondering if the doctor actually killed our Little Inn victims himself or whether the accomplice was indeed the murderer?"

"Oh my, you must be feeling suitably frustrated. Just when I bet you thought the case was closed, heh. What a curve ball. Listen, Susan, are you doing anything right now? I missed my dinner and am ready to pop out to get something to eat. Do you fancy joining me for a bite?"

Susan had herself not eaten other than grabbing a lump of cheese and an apple earlier on. Her stomach rumbled, and she realized that she was starving.

"Yes, I'd love to join you, but where? It's pretty late. I don't think that The Black Dog or The Albion will be still open. What about trying the Japanese restaurant, Drift?"

"Okay, Drift it is. I'll see you in ten minutes then."

THIRTY-FOUR

Susan wondered where Ian lived. To be only ten minutes away meant that he wasn't actually in Goderich, but somewhere in between. She got up and pulled her purse open to see if she had a hairbrush handy and some lipstick. She didn't particularly want to go back home to freshen up, The Lion's Hall washroom would just have to do.

Seven minutes later Susan pulled up outside Drift. The young owner, Peter, was just locking up. Oh no, Susan thought. She jumped out of her car and ran over to him.

"Oh, I was hoping that you would still be open," Susan said breathlessly. "My friend and I are starving, and we just fancied eating here."

The young man smiled and said, "Oh, sure. I'll open up for you."

Susan let out a big sigh of relief. What a charming man and so obliging too!

Ian rolled up just as Susan was sitting down. She had ordered a Sapporo beer and was perusing the menu.

"Hi, Susan," Ian said. He was looking particularly dapper in a casual way wearing jeans and a crisp white shirt with a navy-blue jacket. His blond hair looked freshly washed, and he smelled faintly of some herb Susan couldn't quite identify.

Peter took Ian's drink order, another Sapporo, and they both went back to the menu.

"Oh, I really don't know what to order," Susan said.

"Well, shall we have an order of edamame beans to begin with and what about the tonkatsu? It's like a pork cutlet covered in bread-crumbs. It's very tasty. The beef spareribs are to die for. We could just order the chef's platter and have an extra couple of dishes on the side to share?"

"That sounds perfect." Susan said. She liked a man to take control of ordering for both of them. Henri used to do that all the time, but she had put that down to him being a bit of a food snob and of course, being French.

"So, Ian, where do you live? I know that you're ten minutes away and I know that you work in Goderich, but where exactly is your house?"

Ian was quiet for a bit before answering. "I used to own my own house out on Airport Line. Then my marriage went belly up, and I had to sell it. I briefly rented a place in Goderich and my dad passed away leaving Mom to run the farm on her own.

Two years ago, I moved back home to the old farm on Porters Line. I'm almost embarrassed to say that I live at home with my mother, but she's eighty-five and struggling with poor health. My one brother lives in Alberta and my other brother is in Ottawa so it's really up to me to look after her."

"I know, it's difficult." Susan said. "Both of my parents died ten years ago within one year of each other and so I never had to deal with the aging parent dilemma. It is a real problem. I know so many of my friends are going through similar issues. We're the baby boomer generation."

Ian laughed, "You make it sound like a curse. I actually have enjoyed living with my mom. I've had time to get to know her, you know, as a person and not just a mother."

"But what about entertaining friends, isn't it awkward having people back to your mom's house?"

"Not really and I don't have many friends. I'm what people call a workaholic. The highlight of any day for me is collecting the eggs from our old barn. My parents have always kept a few chickens and they have the run of the barn. I used to love it as a boy hunting down eggs nestled all about the place in the hay. I still love the sense of achievement when I find half a dozen or so eggs and then I can scramble them for our breakfast. It's the farm to table thing."

Their meal came and there was a companionable silence while they both wolfed down their food. It was past ten thirty before they thanked Peter profusely and went to leave the restaurant.

"That was a lovely meal and was just the right thing to take my mind off this messy case. Thank you, Ian."

"Maybe we could do this another time." Ian said as he walked with Susan to her car. "I enjoyed talking to you. By the way, would you like some fresh eggs?"

"I would love some, but there's no hurry, only when you have enough to spare."

"The chickens seem to be dropping lots of eggs right now, so we have loads to spare. I'll drop some off sometime this week."

Susan drove home in deep contemplation. She had, indeed, had a very pleasant evening. She found Ian's company relaxing and undemanding. The fact that he lived with his mother she found rather endearing. Her thoughts, however, were rudely broken by the shrill ring of her cell phone. It was the Toronto Police reporting back.

"Ma'am, we've got Melissa Manson here for questioning, but I have to tell you right now that she was out of the country at the time of both murders. She was living in Florida writing her books and only returned to Canada this year."

Susan thought for a minute before replying. "Thank you, officer.

Could you please ask her if she would consent to providing a DNA swab so we can eliminate her from our enquiry and then let her go home? Thanks so much. Now what about Pippa Hargreaves?"

"Ah, yes, well, there was nobody at her condo, so we contacted her place of work at St. Joseph's Hospital. She had been on duty the previous day working a night shift and wasn't due back to work for a couple of days. We'll keep trying to trace her."

"Right, okay, keep me posted and thank you again."

THIRTY-FIVE

Susan put her phone away and thought to herself that if Pippa was the doctor's accomplice, then there surely would be some evidence in his house to prove the connection. Instead of going straight home she decided to make a short detour to Dr. Glover's house and see if Sergeant Flowers had found any incriminating evidence.

The village was enveloped in a coat of blackness with not a single star in sight. There had been talk of more snow which made Susan's heart flutter as she hated it, but it was positively balmy outside, and no way would it be cold enough to snow. There were few streetlights Susan noted as she drove down Jane Street, to Tuyl, and parked her car alongside Sergeant Flowers in the driveway.

To her surprise, just leaving the house was a very distressed Peggy Grierson. She was visibly crying. Poor woman, Susan thought, she must have just heard about her friend the doctor's death.

She approached Peggy and put her arms around the distraught woman.

"I'm so sorry for your loss, Peggy. I do, however, have a few questions that I would like to ask you."

Peggy sniffed loudly and answered with a broken voice. "He was a good friend to me. When my husband died, he came around every day and sat with me and nursed me through my sorrow. I cannot and will not believe that he murdered those authors at The Little Inn."

"Mrs. Grierson, we know that Dr. Glover had no children, but do you know if he had any nieces or female cousins or if he had any connection to either Melissa Manson or Pippa Hargreaves, the romance writers from the Literary Festival?"

"Why on earth are you asking me these questions? What would any of those women have to do with the murders?" Peggy asked her voice growing stronger.

"Well, we believe that the doctor might have had an accomplice, a female collaborator." Susan replied reluctant to give too much away.

"Let me think a minute," Peggy said and paused a while before answering, "There was a young woman that Janet and the doctor had taken under their wing five or six years ago, about a year before Janet passed away. I really didn't know the Glover's very well then, but when Janet was sick, we became quite close, and she used to talk about this girl as if she was their daughter. In fact, I thought that she was actually their own child, so you can imagine how surprised I was when I found out that she was only a good friend.

"From what I could gather she had met the doctor when he was doing a regular Friday shift at Clinton Hospital in the emergency wing. He used to go there on a rotation with other doctors sharing the load. Janet told me that this woman was a nurse at the hospital. She also told me her name, but I cannot remember it now. There is a photograph on the wall in the lobby which shows the doctor, his wife Janet, and the girl altogether. You will be able to see for yourself if she is someone that you know."

"Thank you, Peggy. Now, have Constable Brown and Elliot paid you a visit yet to take your statement?"

"No. The minute that I heard that Rose Blair was in a coma I drove straight over to the hospital. They wouldn't let me see her as only close family are allowed into the ICU. I didn't know that and so I came straight back here to visit Dr. Glover as I hadn't seen him all day and wanted to ask him if he knew anything about what had happened to Rose. When I got here, the officers told me that the doctor was dead." She started to cry again.

"Well, Peggy, my officers will pay you a visit, but not until tomorrow morning. They will take your statement and, if you don't mind, they will take a quick swab from your mouth to verify DNA. Right, I must be going now. Go home and try to get a good night's sleep, Mrs. Grierson."

Peggy sniffed and walked down the driveway. She only lived around the corner on Glass Street. Susan would send her Constables there in the morning, but it was only after Peggy had gone, that Susan stopped and recalled what the old lady had said.

How on earth did she know that the doctor was responsible for the murders at The Little Inn? Her very words were, I cannot believe that he murdered those authors at The Little Inn. Peggy Grierson definitely knew more than she was letting on.

Susan walked towards the doctor's house and was greeted by Sergeant Flowers in the hallway. She immediately looked at the wall and sure enough a large, framed photograph was mounted exactly where Peggy had said it would be. Bingo, Susan thought, we have her.

"Look, Sergeant," Susan said pointing to the photograph, "Without doubt that young woman standing between the doctor and his wife is Pippa Hargreaves."

"Yes, Ma'am, and look what I found in his desk drawer."

Sergeant Flowers handed a bunch of letters tied together with a yellow ribbon over to Susan.

"I only glanced at the top one but it's obvious to me that Pippa and the doctor enjoyed a very close friendship. I also found this list of names and addresses."

The Sergeant handed a handwritten list over to Susan. She quickly scanned it and immediately saw Chris Saul, Sally Albright,

Matt Irons, James Kidd, and Lynda Barnes names written neatly in a column.

All the names but one had been crossed out. Lynda Barnes name remained uncrossed and glared out at Susan as if a reminder that the there was still a killer at large. But was the doctor's friendship to Pippa Hargreaves sufficient evidence that she was in fact his accomplice?

Susan shook her head. Sadly, they still had no concrete evidence that Pippa was involved in the murders. Until they could get a sampling of her DNA, there was nothing other than a friendship to connect the woman to any of the murders.

"It looks like we've got her, Ma'am," the Sergeant said.

"Hold on, Sergeant, we've yet to apprehend her and then obtain a conclusive DNA result, but yes, it certainly looks as if we've found the connection. Right, we'll call it a night now. It's late and I don't know about you, but I'm exhausted. We'll meet again tomorrow at the briefing in the afternoon. Good night, Sergeant, good work."

THIRTY-SIX

Tom woke up with a start. His neck was cricked and his whole body ached. Sleeping in a chair parked by Rose's bedside, did not make for a fitful night's sleep. The nurse in charge had given him a pillow and a blanket and that had helped a little. He stood up and shook his body like a dog. A cup of coffee was needed, that and a wash.

Tom looked at his watch. It was 7:30 a.m. and the hospital was stirring. Rose lay peacefully tucked into the bed with crisp white sheets folded neatly over her chest. Tom was almost envious of her gentle breathing and deep sleep. Other than a bandage around her head, colour had returned to Rose's face, and she almost looked her old self.

"Good morning, love," Tom said as he bent over to kiss Rose, "Sorry I'm so bristly and unshaven. Look, I'm just popping out for a coffee and sandwich from Tim Horton's. Love you, my darling."

Tom left the hospital and drove one block over to Tim Horton's. On the way there, he passed the Clinton Slots Casino and racetrack. He had never personally been but knew many people who frequented the casino on a regular basis.

The REACH centre adjoined the racetrack. Originally built as a college for equine management it had recently diversified offering other programs and courses in partnership with Fanshawe College in London. Tom wondered if they might eventually offer ESL classes and then Paul could move to Clinton where the housing was much cheaper than in London. Thinking about Paul made Tom reach for his phone. He should call home to see how things were and to make sure that the dogs had been let out.

Paul picked up the phone. "Oh, hi Dad. How's Mom?"

"She's much the same, son. Have you taken the dogs out and given them some kibbles?"

"Dad, stop fretting, everything is fine here. Ally and I are just heading out back to London. We thought that we would swing by the hospital and see Mom and Aunt Kate. Oh, and Jessica's coming over. She said that she would bring you in some lunch."

"Oh, thank you, Paul. It sounds as if you've got everything under control. Look, I must go now. I'll see you soon."

Tom ordered his coffee and sandwich and headed back to the hospital. Before going back to Rose, he decided to go and find Kate and Lynda and see if they had woken up yet from their drugged induced sleep.

Finding a police officer standing outside their room was a bit daunting. Tom wondered why there should be someone guarding the women, from what or whom?

After establishing who he was having shown his driving license to the officer, Tom was allowed into the room where two beds holding Kate and Lynda lay side by side. A nurse was in the room checking out charts. Both women were still out cold. Tom spoke to the nurse, "How much longer before these sleeping beauties wake up?"

"It normally takes up to twenty-four hours and they've been out for the count now for fifteen hours. I would think that by lunch time they might be wide awake."

Tom thanked the nurse and went to leave. Something niggled at him. "Do I know you from somewhere?" Tom said.

The nurse looked startled. "No, no, I've certainly never met you before. You must have me mistaken for someone else."

Just then the doctor came into the room and the nurse left, leaving the doctor and Tom alone together.

"You're Rose Blair's husband, aren't you?" He said to Tom.

"Yes, she's in the ICU. Have you been in to check on her yet?"

The doctor nodded, "Yes, I've just come from her room. No changes, I'm afraid, but you know that she could come out of her coma anytime." He looked at Tom sympathetically. "You should go home and get some rest."

Tom shook his head. "No, I can't leave my wife. I'm alright, really."

"Well, at some stage you'll want to go home and freshen up. Maybe when another family member comes to visit, you could pop home for a bit."

"Yes, that sounds like a plan. Thank you, Doctor."

Tom left the room and returned to Rose. Maybe when Jessica came, he would go home to clean himself up and stay with Ben and Puff for a bit.

THIRTY-SEVEN

Susan had barely slept a wink. After getting home she had sat up to the wee hours of the morning reading the pile of letters Sergeant Flowers had found in the doctor's desk.

The tone of the letters was loving, but not at all intimate. There was no sense of a sexual relationship, instead the letters were chatty and personal, like a daughter to a father.

The earliest of the letters dated back to just after the doctor's wife, Janet, had died. Pippa, or Philippa as she signed her name, was full of sorrow, promising to come down to help him get through the awfulness of mourning a loved one.

The following letter clearly stated her intention to help the doctor in his mission to avenge his wife's death. It was clear too that Philippa blamed the stress of the huge financial loss as being a catalyst for the cancer that had taken Janet away.

The letters got steadily more paranoiac as Pippa made plans to help the doctor eliminate the DFI team.

Susan looked at the post marks on the envelopes. There were half a dozen letters mailed from London and another half a dozen mailed from Guelph. The rest were from Toronto.

Were the letters proof enough to convict her? Susan thought as she tied the big bundle up and prepared to go to bed. Absolutely no where in any of the letters had she actually referred to the murders. She had obliquely made references to mission accomplished, and still researching, but no actual names had been mentioned in any of the letters to Dr. Glover. Unfortunately, there would not be enough in the letters to implicate her to any of the murders, Susan thought. DNA would probably be the only way, short of an actual confession from Pippa herself.

Susan yawned and got into bed. What a day, she thought, what an awful day it had been. She turned out the bedside light and attempted to sleep.

THIRTY-EIGHT

At 7:30 a.m. Susan got up, dressed, grabbed a quick cup of coffee and a piece of toast, and rushed out of the house to where Constable Ryan was waiting for her in the parking lot.

"Well, Constable, there is no point in us driving all the way to Toronto. Melissa Manson has been questioned and a DNA swab taken, but Pippa Hargreaves has gone AWOL. What I would like us to do is to drive to London and Guelph and talk to some of her employers. She worked at Victoria Hospital in London for two years and at Memorial Hospital in Guelph for three years. Prior to that, she was working at Clinton Hospital. I would also like, if we have time, to interview her parents whom I believe live in Waterloo. Right, we've got a fair amount of driving to do, and we have to be back in Bayfield for our two o'clock meeting. Do you want to drive or should I?"

Constable Ryan had been a passenger in DCI Parker's car before and it had quite frankly terrified her. The Chief drove like a maniac at speeds that she herself had never reached. She eagerly agreed to drive, and they set off for London with Constable Ryan at the wheel.

The residents of Bayfield had woken up that morning to a

winter's wonderland with a light covering of snow over everything like icing on a cake. The roads, however, were as slick as ice and Constable Ryan had to drive slow and steadily. She could see that DCI Parker was getting more and more impatient with her driving, so she reluctantly put her foot down. They reached London in record time, fifty minutes, although by the time they got to the hospital it was over an hour, but it was still only 8:30 a.m. Susan had telephoned from the car to the human resource department. When they arrived, they were shown into a small office and the HR manager came in to greet them.

"So, officers, how can I be of assistance to you?" The tall, well groomed, and efficient woman asked as she politely held out her hand to be shaken. "My name is Sharon, Sharon Lewington. How can I help you?"

"We believe a Pippa, or Philippa Hargreaves, worked at the hospital sometime during the period of 2012 and 2014. Do you have a record of her employment and is there anyone you know whom might have known her during that period?"

Sharon Lewington frowned before answering. "I can help you with the first part of your request although normally this information would be strictly out of bounds, but I assume this is part of some police enquiry?"

"Yes, it is and thank you for your cooperation." Susan answered relieved that the woman had not demanded a court order to release private information and to which she would have been perfectly entitled.

They waited ten minutes and could hear the tapping of the computer keyboard. Sharon Lewington returned carrying a printed sheet of paper.

"So, here we have her record of employment. It appears that she worked in the paediatric ward for two years, was a diligent nurse and received no complaints from either any of the doctors or patients.

There is only one comment here that says that Nurse Hargreaves left suddenly with no notice."

Susan interrupted her, "Do you have an actual date that she left her employment at the hospital?"

Sharon smiled and said, "Yes, it was August 14th, 2014, actually my birthday."

Susan thought quickly. That was the day after James Kidd had been found murdered.

"One more question, do you know if Nurse Hargreaves had access to drugs?"

The manager's eyebrows shot up. "Well, the patients are all on medications prescribed by the resident doctor here in the hospital. So, yes, all the nurses have access to drugs in the wards. Is this to do with opiates and the drug market by any chance?"

"We are not at liberty to discuss the case, but no, we are not investigating a drug scandal or anything like that."

The manager's demeanour altered perceptively. "Is there anything else I can help you with? I do have a nine o'clock meeting scheduled today."

Susan shook her head, "No, you've been more than helpful. Thank you."

Constable Ryan and DCI Parker left the hospital and started on their journey to Guelph.

"Ma'am, should we go to Waterloo first as it's a bit closer and just off the highway?"

"Yes, I'll give the Hargreaves a call just to make sure they are going to be in."

Susan struck lucky and made an appointment to visit them in an hour's time.

They drove along in silence while Susan read up her notes on the Hargreaves. There wasn't much in the file. To all extensive purposes they were a normal, hard-working family. The mother, a teacher, and the father, an electrician. They had two children, Pippa and a younger son who was also an electrician.

They pulled up outside a respectable ranch-style house. A woman wearing grey pants and a bright yellow sweater answered the door. The resemblance to her daughter was striking. She had a slightly elfin looking face with big blue eyes and a ready smile. Her husband, Pippa's father, looked much older than his wife, maybe it was the grey hair, but he appeared haggard and tired. The two of them glanced enquiringly at Susan.

"Oh, I beg your pardon," Mrs. Hargreaves said. "I'm forgetting my manners. Do please come in."

They walked into a small lobby that lead, up a few stairs, to a large, sunny living room. It overlooked a fair sized, fenced in garden which even in the winter Susan could see was a well cared for lot.

"So, how can we help you?" Pippa's mother asked still looking at them with a worried look etched all over her face.

The father spoke first with a deep sonorous voice. "Is it about Philippa?"

Susan nodded and said, "Do you mind if we sit down for a minute? I've got a few questions to ask you about your daughter."

"She's alright?" Mrs. Hargreaves said with worry creeping up into her voice. "She hasn't done anything wrong, I hope?"

"At this stage we're not sure. Do you know where your daughter is right now?"

"No, but I spoke to her the other day after she got back from her speaking engagement in Bayfield. That would be Sunday evening. She said that she was working at the hospital on Monday. Other than that, I'm not sure where she could be right now."

"Do you know a Doctor Glover from Bayfield?"

Mrs. Hargreaves cocked her head to one side reminding Susan of a pigeon.

"Why do you ask?"

"Well, we believe that your daughter had formed a close relationship with the man. Do you know anything about this?"

Once again the bird-like head movement and then Mrs. Hargreaves sighed and said, "Our daughter is obsessive compulsive, not with objects, but with people. She would form almost obsessively close relationships with friends when she was a little girl and it always ended up in tears. I believe that Philippa attached herself to the doctor in this way to the extent that she fantasized that he was a father to her. Yes, we knew about her friendship, but there was nothing that we could do about it. Why do you ask? Has anything happened to the doctor?"

"I'm sorry to have to tell you, but the doctor is dead."

Mrs. Hargreaves face fell, "You don't mean Philippa...?"

"No, he took his own life, but we are looking for your daughter over another matter. Do you have any idea as to where she might have gone?"

"You know, when Philippa was in a relationship, she excluded everyone from her life. She has no friends left."

"What about her brother? What's his name?"

"Simon. No, Simon lives in Toronto with his wife Becky. He's never been close to his sister. He would be the last person that she would go to."

"Do you own a cottage or a second home somewhere?"

"Yes, well we do have a family cottage just south of the village of Bayfield. It's down Centennial Road. Mind you, it's not winterized so I doubt very much that she would go there this time of the year."

"We'll take the address down all the same. Can you think of anywhere else that she might go?"

"Possibly Sarnia, my sister lives there and Philippa has always been quite close to her aunt. I'm not sure where else she might go. Can't you tell me what this is all about?"

"Sorry, we're not at liberty to discuss the case with you, Mrs. Hargreaves. But thank you for all your help."

DCI Parker and Constable Ryan got up to leave.

"Do please tell us if our daughter is in any trouble." Mrs. Hargreaves pleaded. Her husband intervened quickly.

"Now, Nell, the officers have already told you as much as they can." He turned to them and said, "I'll show you to the front door."

They had just reached the front door when Susan suddenly remembered something,

"Mrs. Hargreaves, do you have a hairbrush or toothbrush belonging to your daughter? It is really important that we can try to eliminate her from our investigation with DNA testing."

Mrs. Hargreaves nodded and went upstairs to see what she could find. She returned a few minutes later with a hairbrush and a comb.

"Will these do?" She said and handed them over to DCI Parker.

"Yes, that's great and once again thank you."

Before they left Mr. Hargreaves said in a quiet voice, not loud enough for his wife to hear,

"Our Philippa has real mental health issues." With that he nodded farewell with great sadness in his eyes. He firmly closed the door behind them.

They drove off in silence until Susan said, "Okay, last port of call Guelph and then it's back to Bayfield. Do you want to grab a cup of coffee from Tim Horton's before we hit the highway?"

They pulled into a Tim Horton's drive-through and both ordered a coffee to go and a bagel with cream cheese. It would be at least three hours before they would be back in Bayfield.

THIRTY-NINE

essica arrived to relieve Tom at ten o'clock that morning. She bought a basket containing a thermos flask of carrot and ginger soup, some fresh crusty bread, and a small quiche. There was a Tupperware container filled with brownies, homemade cookies, and a couple of pieces of fruit. After chatting with Jessica a little while, Tom decided to go back home to shower, shave, and generally freshen up.

"Call me, Jess, if there's any change in your mother, even the slightest bit. Look, I'll be back at the most in an hour."

"Dad, stop worrying. Mom will be fine. I've bought a book of poems that I thought I'd read to her. You go and relax awhile."

Tom reluctantly left the room. He felt bad leaving Rose. Popping out for a quick coffee was one thing but going home and being gone for an hour was a little long for his comfort.

Puff and Ben were ecstatic to see him. Tom could barely move with both dogs barking and jumping up and down with delight. He finally walked into the kitchen. Paul and Ally had left it quite tidy although remnants of their meal remained still on the table. Sitting next to a plate of lemon squares lay the programme from The Little Inn's Literary Festival.

It seemed an age since Rose and he had attended the Dinner with the Author crime writers evening, Tom thought as he glanced at the photographs of all five authors. It was so sad to think that two of the writers were now dead. Suddenly Tom stiffened. He looked at the programme more carefully. Yes, he was almost certain that he was right in thinking that one of the romance writers was indeed none other than the nurse whom he had seen in Lynda and Kate's room at the hospital.

Tom studied the publicist's photograph of Pippa Hargreaves. Yes, she was definitely the same woman he had seen earlier that day. But, how strange, Tom thought, that one of the authors from the Literary Festival should be a nurse at Clinton Hospital, particularly because Pippa Hargreaves' biography stated that she lived in Toronto. He mulled it over in his mind and then decided that he would call Susan Parker after he had freshened up. Maybe it was nothing, but it seemed just too much of a coincidence and Tom didn't believe in coincidences.

Twenty minutes later Tom had showered, shaved, cleaned his teeth, and put fresh clothes on. He felt like a new man again after having felt so grungy for over a day. It was amazing how dirty one felt even after a comparatively short time.

Tom was about to take the dogs for a short walk around the block when he remembered to phone Susan. He would make his phone call before going out. Tapping in her cell number Tom wondered how the investigation was going. Maybe he might be able to ask Susan exactly what had gone on in Lynda and Barry Forbes house that afternoon when Rose had been kicked so badly in the head.

"DCI Parker speaking."

"Hi Susan, it's me, Tom. Look, I need to talk to you about something."

"Tom, I'm on the road right now. I'll be back in Bayfield around

1:30 p.m. Is it urgent? What's the problem? It's not about Rose, is it?"

"Well, it's not urgent, just a strange coincidence. There was a nurse in Lynda and Kate's room this morning and I swear that she was Pippa Hargreaves, you know, the romance writer. Anyway, she was dressed in a nurse's tunic and pants. I just thought that you might like to know, that's all."

There was a stunned silence the other end of the line and then Susan spoke sharply. "Tom, listen, this is very important, was there a police officer outside guarding the women's room?"

"Oh, yes and he was quite officious to me. He demanded to see my I.D. Why do you ask?"

"What was the nurse doing, Tom?"

"Well, I think that she was reading their charts and then the doctor came in and she left the room."

"Okay, thank you. One last thing, are you going back to the hospital?"

"Yes, I just popped home to freshen up. Why do you ask?"

"Tom, I would like you to speak to the officer guarding the room and tell him about the nurse and what she looks like. Under no circumstances can that same nurse be allowed into Kate and Lynda's room again. She could be our murderer."

"What?" Tom exclaimed, "What on earth is going on?"

"Tom, I can't explain right now. I'll tell you everything soon. I promise."

Tom put the phone down feeling somewhat perplexed. Just what was going on? Pippa Hargreaves the murderer? He had thought that Doctor Glover had been involved, well at least from what he had gathered, the doctor had kicked Rose for some inexplicable reason, and then he had taken his own life.

Susan Parker had a lot of explaining to do, but right now Tom had other things on his mind. He needed to get back to his darling wife and now.

FORTY

"Right, Constable, forget about Guelph, head right back to Bayfield. Pippa has been seen at Clinton Hospital which means she's still in the area."

"Ma'am, does that mean she's come back to finish the job that Doctor Glover failed?"

"You mean to kill Lynda Forbes? Yes, I'm afraid so. It certainly looks that way. Now, officer, for God sakes pull over and let me drive!" Susan shouted impatiently.

They were back in Bayfield by 1:00 p.m. Susan debated whether to drive over to Clinton Hospital right away but thought better of it. Security had been vamped up and everyone would be on the look out for Pippa. No, she needed to gather her team together and make a plan, but first Constable Ryan and she would pop into The Black Dog for a quick bite to eat.

The pub was teaming with people. They managed to get a table for two in the back corner of the restaurant. Both of them ordered soft drinks and fish and chips. Susan tried to relax, but inside her heart was beating fast and her adrenalin was flowing. They were onto the final chase, and she could almost smell the blood.

Susan just knew that the game was up for Pippa. It was only a matter of time now before they would have her hauled in for questioning. Just then the phone rang breaking Susan's train of thought and bringing her back to reality with a start.

"DCI Parker speaking."

"Ian here. Look, I've just finished the autopsy on Doctor Glover and thought that you might be interested to know that the man had only a short time to live. His body was shot through with cancer."

"Would he have known that he was a dying man?" Susan asked.

"Most certainly. I'm just surprised that he was able to function as well as he did. No signs of chemo in his blood. I guess that he knew that it was too far gone for any treatment."

"Any news on the DNA tests taken from Chris Saul and Sally Albright?"

"I've chased them up and requested a special fast track. They promised to get the results to me by tomorrow."

"That's great. Thank you so much."

Susan was about to say goodbye when Ian added, "By the way, I've got some eggs for you."

"Thank you, Ian. Would you like me to pick them up?"

"No, I'm often in Bayfield. I thought that maybe you might like to have dinner with me again soon. What about Saturday?"

Susan suddenly felt a pang of guilt about Peter Joyce. She hadn't seen him all week. She should be having dinner with him and not Ian.

"I can't do dinner this week. Maybe next week. Look, I'll be in touch."

Susan put her phone down and smiled at Constable Ryan. "My complicated love life. Are you married or do you have a boyfriend?"

Constable Ryan looked a bit taken aback by the personal question, and then she regained her composure quickly.

"Yes, ma'am, I have a boyfriend. He's in London and I do miss him. I've been staying at The Ashwood this week and I'm really looking forward to seeing him when this investigation gets wound up."

Susan felt awfully guilty. She had never really thought about her team and the sacrifices they made often working away from home and leaving their loved one's behind. She knew that the statistics on split marriages showed that one in two marriages in the police force, half of them, never made it and she was not at all surprised. It quite saddened her and once again she had second thoughts about her retirement. This time she might jolly well retire for good.

"Well, eat up now and then let's get going. It's crunch time, I can feel it in my bones. I want to get this case wrapped up and soon." Susan said a tad impatiently.

"Here's to that," Constable Ryan said and tucked into her meal with gusto.

The team was assembled and waiting. There was a general air of anticipation and Susan knew that she had to keep up the pace and energy to finish the job.

"Listen up, everyone. Pippa Hargreaves was seen at Clinton Hospital. We now know that she's in the area. We just have to close the net. Now, Sergeant Flowers, did you learn anything from Peggy Grierson that we don't already know?"

The Sergeant smiled, "You were right, Ma'am, she knew more than she was letting on. For instance, the doctor had taken her into his confidence and told her about his plan to eliminate the DFI team responsible for his financial loss. She said that she honestly did not believe him, she never dreamt that he would follow through with his plan. In fact, she was pretty emphatic that it was all just talk on his part, however, she had a few things to say about Pippa Hargreaves."

"Go on, Sergeant, we're all ears." Susan said.

"Well, Peggy knew about Pippa's attachment to Doctor Glover, and she found it quite disturbing, but she thinks that the poor woman definitely has mental health issues. She actually wondered whether

Pippa Hargreaves was psychopathic. Anyway, she said that she overheard the doctor talking to Pippa on the phone. He mentioned the names Chris Saul and Sally Albright and then what followed was an argument of sorts. Obviously, Peggy could only hear the one side of the conversation, but she said that the doctor shouted, 'No, don't do it.'"

Susan interrupted the Sergeant, "Did she say when this argument took place?"

Sergeant Flowers continued, "Yes, Ma'am, it was the middle of last week, a couple of days before the Literary Festival at The Little Inn."

"Thank you, okay, now that's interesting. I think that we are beginning to get a clearer picture of our prime suspect. Until we get the DNA results back from the lab, we won't know conclusively whether the doctor was our killer or Pippa Hargreaves. We have her definitely down for the murders of James Kidd and Matt Irons. It could just be that she committed all four murders herself. Whatever, she has to be apprehended and fast. So, here's the plan.

Sergeant Flowers, I would like you and Constable Ryan to check out the Hargreaves family cottage down Centennial Road. Do we know what car she's driving?"

Constable Ryan shot up her hand, "Yes, ma'am, I've just checked with our database, and she's registered as driving a white Toyota Corolla, registration number AWOL 369.

"Thank you, Constable Ryan. I would like you two to just watch her movements from a comfortable distance, that's assuming she's actually at the cottage. Constables Elliot and Brown, I want you to drive to Sarnia and talk to Sharon Hargreaves's sister, Pippa's aunt. It might be where Pippa is staying."

Susan's telephone rang sharply. She hated being interrupted during a briefing, but when she saw the name of the caller, she decided to take the call.

"DCI Parker speaking."

It was a very agitated Sharon Hargreaves. Her voice sounded strained as if she had been crying.

"You asked me to call if I remembered anything else significant. Well, Philippa had an obsessive relationship with a fellow nurse. It was while she was working at Clinton Hospital around six years ago. The nurse was called Suzy Ball. The reason why I remembered is that nurse had to take out a restraining order on Philippa. Then, our daughter published her first romance novel called, The Sins of Sexy Suzy, and Suzy Ball went ballistic. She threatened to sue Philippa, and it all got pretty nasty. Philippa moved to London and the whole thing blew over. The reason why I'm mentioning this is that Suzy Ball lives not far from Bayfield on Goshen Line, really only a stone's throw from our cottage. Philippa might be there. I don't know, but it's worth a try."

"Thank you, Mrs. Hargreaves. I know that this must be difficult for you but thank you for your help."

Susan put the phone down and turned to her team.

"Okay, Constables Elliot and Brown, change of plan. I want you to find this Suzy Ball and see if there is a white Toyota parked in her driveway. Do not, I repeat, do not do anything until you have reported back to me. Okay, go to it everyone and keep the communications open."

FORTY-ONE

Sergeant Flowers and Constable Ryan drove in companionable silence down Highway 21 to Centennial Road, where they took a right turn and drove towards the lake. The cottage was not hard to find, but it was apparently obvious right away, that there was nobody living there. Indeed, it looked as if it had been closed up for the winter. Constable Ryan called DCI Parker and told her what they had found.

"Should we go and knock on the door, Ma'am?"

"No but see if you can find any neighbours and ask around if anyone has seen Pippa Hargreaves in the vicinity. When you've done that drive up to Goshen Line and meet with Constables Brown and Elliot. And Constable, be careful."

The two officers canvassed the area around Centennial Road and only found one homeowner who lived there all year round. Most of the cottages were owned by summer folk.

Mr. Arthur Widen said that he had seen a white Toyota Corolla parked outside the Hargreaves cottage a couple of nights ago. He had been walking his dogs at around ten o'clock at night and had observed a light on in the cottage and saw a car in the driveway. It was gone the next day.

They drove back to the Highway and headed towards St. Josephs. Sergeant Flowers was approaching the turn off for Zurich, on the left past the Catholic Church, when P.C. Ryan shouted, "Stop, look, there in the church car park."

Sure enough, a white Toyota Corolla was parked close to the side of the church towards the back of the car park. Sergeant Flowers did a quick U turn and drove to where the car sat conspicuously, all by itself.

"Maybe there were other cars parked here. It does seem odd to see her car just left so openly in an empty car park." Constable Ryan said.

"So, it's been abandoned then," Susan said after they had called it in. "Go and ask the tenants of those apartments next to the church and see if anyone saw Pippa."

Sergeant Flowers and Constable Ryan knocked on the first door of what must have been originally St. Josephs Catholic School now converted into four apartments.

An old man answered the door. "My, that was quick," he said. "I just got off the phone reporting my car missing. I'm impressed."

The two officers looked at each other as it dawned on them what had just happened. Pippa Hargreaves now had car theft to add to her criminal charges.

"Right, sir, remind us again what your car looks like, the make, registration number, and anything that you can think to tell us." Constable Ryan went to write the details in her notebook.

"It's a green Volvo, 1998, license plate AJXY 698. Look, I want it back and soon. You try living here in the middle of no where without four wheels."

He did have a valid point, D.C. Ryan thought, although St. Josephs historically had always been somewhat isolated. First there had been a small enclave of French Catholics, so poor that none of them could own any land and they relied on fishing as their mainstay.

Then there had been the grandiose schemer, Narcisse Canton, who envisioned a canal connecting Lake Erie to Lake Huron. Investors lost thousands of dollars when the whole project folded, partially due to the turmoil in Europe with rumblings of the WW1, but also because Narcisse, himself, went bankrupt. Ironically, St. Joseph's presently supported some of the biggest and most affluent houses in Southwestern Ontario. It certainly no longer was the poor relation of Ontario.

Sergeant Flowers and Constable Ryan drove up into the village of Zurich. It probably was a pretty place in the summer, and she had read about the Bean Festival, but right now, Constable Ryan thought, still clothed in winter, the village looked bleak and not very welcoming.

Sergeant Flowers turned left onto Goshen Line opposite the Bluewater Medical centre and past the relatively new Zurich Public Library on the corner. Goshen Line ran along what they called The Huron Ridge. The whole area from The Ridge to the lake had once been a glacial moraine and as such had been identified as a potentially excellent area to cultivate vines.

Constable Ryan had noticed a small vineyard just south of the village of Bayfield and she had heard that there was a large winery called Dark Horse, in Grand Bend next to the Huron Playhouse. There was also a lovely well-established winery just north of Clinton called Maelstrom. In a few years time, Constable Ryan thought, the whole area could end up similar to Prince Edward County, a fine destination for wine tasting. She would definitely come back to visit the area again next summer.

CONSTABLES BROWN and Elliot accessed the 911 database and retrieved the address of Suzy Ball. They drove to what appeared to be a small, stone farmhouse. As they approached the driveway, it was apparent that they had company.

There were two cars parked side by side, one a dark green Volvo and another, a brown Subaru. There was no white Toyota Corolla in sight. Constable Elliot contacted DCI Parker.

"Ma'am, we're at Suzy Ball's house, but there is no sign of Pippa Hargreaves' vehicle."

"Is there a dark green Volvo, Constable?"

"Yes, the Volvo and another car, a Subaru."

"Right, officers, standby but do not approach the house. Sergeant Flowers and Constable Ryan are on their way and so am I."

FORTY-TWO

Jessica had noticed that her mother's eyelids had been fluttering like the tiny heartbeat of a small sparrow. She had held her hand and talked to her about Abby and Ella and how Ella hadn't dropped the subject of Cyril the Squirrel. She was still indignant that she had not been able to see him, and Abby had continued to tease her sister by saying that the squirrel was just for babies and so it went on.

Jessica told her mother that Puff and Ben were just fine, and that Tom had gone home to shower and how he had really smelt rank and she laughed and squeezed her mother's hand again. It was then that she first noticed the fluttering of Rose's eyelids. I know that she can hear every word that I'm saying, Jessica thought, and continued to chat away about the girls and what their plans were for the summer.

Tom returned within the hour. He certainly looked one hundred percent better. It was amazing what a good clean up could do. Before she left, Jessica kissed her mom and told her how much she loved her. Hugging Tom, she told him to watch Rose's eyelids.

"Dad, I'm going to check in on Aunty Kate and mom's friend before I head back to London."

"Do me a favour, love," Tom said. "If the two sleeping beauties have woken up, can you pop back to let me know?"

Jessica left and walked to the elevator to take her to the room where Kate and Lynda had been assigned. She was surprised to see a very officious looking police officer standing in front of the door.

"No visitors are allowed, miss." He said and folded his arms across his Kevlar clad chest revealing a gun nestled in a side strapped holster. Jessica wondered whether it was a real gun or a taser, whatever, the whole effect was undeniably threatening. I sure wouldn't want to cross this guy, she thought as she backed away and fairly bumped into a doctor coming up behind her.

"Oops, I'm sorry," Jessica said and added quickly, "are you about to visit my Aunt Kate? I was told no visitors are allowed, but my dad and I are anxious to know how they both are doing."

The doctor smiled at Jessica, "I can tell you that they are both wide awake and none the worse for the experience. They have absolutely no memory of being drugged, although they both remember going shopping and having lunch together in Goderich."

"Can I see them?" Jessica asked.

"I'm sorry, but the answer is no. We're under strict instructions to keep both women safe and secure until told otherwise."

"Oh, well, can you at least give them my love?" Jessica said.

"Will, do, now I really must be getting on." The doctor said and left Jessica wondering what on earth was going on. Maybe her father might have some answers, she thought as she headed back to the ICU.

Tom was thrilled to hear that Kate and Lynda were fine, but equally perplexed to the enforced security. Susan Parker had much explaining to do. In the meantime, though, he had seen, like Jessica, an increased fluttering of Rose's eyelids and at one stage, her right finger had wiggled up and down.

FORTY-THREE

Susan arrived at the Goshen Line farmhouse ten minutes later. There had been no sightings of Pippa Hargreaves yet, but the stolen car, presumed to be appropriated by the suspect, was certainly an indication that she was there.

Before she could mobilize the SWAT team, Susan needed to assess the situation more closely. There was no point in calling in the troops if Pippa and Suzy were just having a friendly chat. But, if there was any indication that the owner of the home or her husband had been compromised in any way, then Susan would make that call to the SWAT team immediately.

She approached the front door with caution, telling her team to stay back and to not look threatening, however, they should remain on alert. Sergeant Flowers had been sent to scope out the back of the stone farmhouse and see if there was a rear entry.

Susan knocked on the front door loudly and waited. Nothing. She was about to turn away when the door creaked open a few inches. She could see Pippa Hargreaves the other side of the door. Her face looked deranged, her large eyes darted here and then.

"Pippa," Susan said, "we need to talk to you."

Suddenly the door was flung wide open, and Susan was able to see inside to a small, old fashioned sitting room. A young woman was strapped to an up right chair. Her mouth was gagged, and her hands and legs tied together with rope. The poor woman's eyes pleaded with Susan's to help her.

"What have you done, Pippa?" Susan said in a conciliatory tone of voice. The last thing she wanted to do was enrage her. "Why have you tied up this innocent woman?"

Suddenly Pippa lurched forward. A syringe with an exposed needle lay in her hand with the plunger pulled back ready for action. She shrieked like a wild banshee to Susan, "Come any nearer and I'll plunge this into Suzy's neck."

So much for the gentle approach, Susan thought. "Okay, calm yourself down. What do you want, Pippa? What do you want us to do?"

"I want you to leave me alone, just go away."

"If we go away, will you let Suzy go?" Susan said, thinking to herself that she really needed a police negotiator on site. There was definitely a technique in negotiating with hostage takers. Unfortunately, the nearest negotiator was in London. She would have to keep Pippa talking and then maybe, just maybe, she might be able to calm the situation down.

"So where is Suzy's husband right now?"

Pippa snarled, "That jerk, he's never here. He's a truck driver and won't be back for at least a week, by which time we'll be long gone."

"Where are you going, Pippa? Or do you like to be called Philippa?"

"What are you on about? Now get off this property before I call the police." Pippa snarled.

"We are the police. Now, put that syringe down and come with me."

Pippa's face altered again. Her features were as fluid as water and changed like the wind. Right now, she had puckered up her forehead and sucked in her cheeks. Her eyes darted to and fro, reminding Susan of a lizard, reptilian, and mean.

"Come on, who do you think I am? What do you take me for? I call the shots here, not you. Now you listen to me, this is what we're going to do. I'm going to get Suzy into the car and we're both going to drive off together. Got it?"

Susan knew that Sergeant Flowers was working his way around the back of the house. She prayed that the element of surprise would not shock Pippa into plunging the syringe into Suzy's neck or, like the doctor, injecting herself.

"Okay, okay, calm down. You can take Suzy into the car. I'll clear the way for you. Officers stand down."

Pippa looked around the outside of the house like a mad woman. Suddenly, she turned to Susan and shrieked.

"There's one officer missing. I counted four policemen before and now there are only three. Where is he?"

Susan could see the silhouette of Sergeant Flowers outlined on the back of the glass kitchen door. She had to keep Pippa engaged in conversation a while longer.

"So, tell me about your love for Suzy? I hear that you even wrote a romance novel after her. The Sins of Sexy Suzy."

Once again Pippa's face changed. This time the grimace was replaced with something close to pride. Yes, Susan thought, tap into her vanity and she might just be able to divert her train of thought.

"Well yes, I did model my story on Suzy. The novel happened to become a best seller and got me started on my writing career."

"But I also heard that Suzy wanted to sue you for defamation of character?"

"Oh, that was just silly melodrama. She really loved the fame it brought to her."

Susan knew that it was now or never. Sergeant Flowers was ready, in place, just waiting for a cue from her.

Suzy Ball's eyes bored down into Susan's.

Susan shouted, "One more time! Pippa, throw down the syringe!"

Susan leapt forward just as Sergeant Flowers rushed through from the kitchen. He had his taser gun out and ready.

Pippa plunged forward towards Suzy with the syringe aimed at her neck, her arm raised in an arc. Sergeant Flowers zapped his taser and Pippa's body arched and convulsed as her whole body succumbed to the stun. The syringe dropped to the ground and Susan grabbed it while Sergeant Flowers deftly handcuffed Pippa.

"Well, done Sergeant," Susan said. "Constable Ryan, put this syringe in an evidence bag and then come and help me over here."

"Constables Brown and Elliot, search the house." Susan walked over to where Suzy, still tied up and gagged, gently sobbed with relief.

Susan untied the gag and the rope that had tied both her hands and legs together. She noticed a long, red rope burn on her legs, but Suzy was unaware of it. She tried to stand up but fell backwards on to the chair.

"Oh, thank you, thank you, you saved my life. She's totally mad, you know, crazy." Suzy sobbed.

"Suzy, is it true that your husband is a truck driver and that he's not here at the moment?"

Suzy's face had been positively beaming, but it now grew serious at the mention of her husband.

"Oh, yes, thank God he wasn't here. I shudder to think what she would have done to him."

She started to physically shake and wrapped her arms around herself as she took a deep breath.

"You do know that she is mentally unstable?"

Susan nodded.

"Seven years ago, I had to take out a restraining order. She wouldn't stop bugging me. That was before I met my husband. She had this massive crush on me and declared that she couldn't live without me. We were working together at Clinton Hospital then."

Susan knew that it was good for survivors to talk and so she let Suzy continue talking without any interruptions.

"Go, on, Suzy. I'm listening."

"Well, at first I enjoyed her company. She was fun, and we laughed a lot together. We used to go to the movie theatre or out to dinner on our days off from work. There was never anything sexual. It began to get creepy when she would just turn up at my house sometimes in the middle of the night and ask if she could stay. At first, I didn't mind as I used to get lonely out here all by myself. My parents moved to Florida ten years ago and left me the house to live in. It's really their home, but it saves me paying rent. So I didn't mind Pippa coming over now and then, but then she suggested that she move in with me. That's when all the trouble started. I didn't want her to move in and the minute that I resisted, she started to get clingier and more demanding, to the point that she would follow me everywhere I went. I think the term is stalking. Even when I would go to visit my gran, I would see her car parked down the road and my grandma lives in Exeter. In the end, I called the police."

Susan interrupted Suzy. "Where was Pippa staying during this time?"

"She stayed at her parent's cottage on Centennial Road in the summer months, but she took a room at a boarding house near the hospital during the winter months."

"Did she ever mention a Doctor Glover?"

"Oh, yes, that's the funny thing. After the police warned her to keep away from me, I had left Clinton Hospital by then and was nursing at Exeter hospital, but I heard that Pippa had latched onto Doctor Glover. He only worked at the hospital on Fridays, but apparently Pippa and the doctor became good friends. I did hear that he had lost his wife. I think that she died of cancer or something like that. You know, in a way, I felt happy for Pippa as she had finally found someone else to love."

"Well, that's very generous of you to say that particularly as Pippa was going to kill you."

Suzy shivered again and Susan realized that shock was setting in. Sergeant Flowers had taken Pippa Hargreaves off to the police cruiser where she would be read her rights before being taken to London to be arraigned. But what to do with the young woman before her, Susan thought.

"Suzy, do you think that we should call your gran? You need to be with someone tonight. We can't leave you alone. Constable Ryan will make you some tea or coffee, but I really would like you to stay with someone just for a little while."

Suzy smiled and nodded her head. "Yes, I'll go and call Gran right away. Thank you for being so concerned. You've been so kind. I really do feel much better now."

"Okay, right, well we'll be off now. Constable Ryan will stay and take your full statement. Here is my card. If you need to talk to me or indeed anyone, and if you remember something else pertaining to Pippa Hargreaves, don't hesitate to call."

"Thank you, thank you." Suzy said as she turned to go back inside with Constable Ryan.

"That was a close call," DCI Parker said to her team. "Good work everyone. We'll be having a debriefing tomorrow morning, but right now go home and get a good rest. You've all deserved it."

The team departed and Susan climbed wearily into her car to drive back to Bayfield. It was time for a stiff drink and some R and R for her at last.

FORTY-FOUR

After Jessica left, Tom sat on the chair beside the bed where Rose lay still in a coma. He took one of her hands and gently squeezed it in his.

"Jess has gone, love, and Kate and Lynda are just fine. All we want now is for you to wake up out of your deep sleep. Would you like to hear some music? I brought in this old C.D. player of mine and found some of your favourite music. Remember the group Bread? We used to sing at the top of our voices, If a Picture Paints a Thousand Words. Oh, you used to love that song. Well, I thought that we could both listen to it, and it will be like a trip down memory lane, love. Oh, and I also bought some John Denver music. Remember Annie's Song?

Rose's eyelids flickered and her lips parted as if she was trying to talk. Tom kissed her gently.

"My love, do you remember that Robert Browning poem?

Grow old with me,

The best is yet to be...

Rose flickered open one eye and her lips began to smile. Then she slowly opened her other eye and looked directly at Tom,

"Oh, Tom Blair, I love you so much." She whispered and tried to sit up in bed but fell back on to her pillow still too weak to do anything other than smile at Tom and let huge, glistening tears roll down her cheeks.

Tom gathered Rose up into his arms and hugged her tightly. He felt his eyes well up and his heart constrict with joy.

"My love, my love, you're back. I can't believe it. You're back!"

FORTY-FIVE

Susan slept like a baby. For the first time in a week, really since the investigation had started, she could feel her body relaxing. She hadn't realized quite how stressed out she had been feeling until she had driven home from Suzy's house and had collapsed into a chair and then had poured herself out a stiff scotch.

Then, and only then, did the realization dawn on Susan that the case could finally be closed. Checking through her emails a while later she had found a note sent to her from Doctor Green, the egg man, as she now thought of him.

With full forensics report back from the lab including DNA results, he had really put pressure to speed up the process and that had paid off, because not only had they tested DNA from the doctor but also had managed to get DNA from the hairbrush Susan had obtained from Pippa's mother.

They had confirmed the correlation of the DNA results from Chris Saul and Sally Albright to the sample taken from Pippa and it was undeniable proof of murder. Not only that, but the DNA markers taken from the cold cases, Matt Irons and James Kidd, also matched the sample. The case could definitely be closed with no loopholes attached.

When Susan woke up the following morning the whole house appeared muffled and silent as a lamb. She looked outside her bedroom window and shook her head with disbelief. The ground was clothed in a heavy blanket of snow. Big, fat snowflakes were steadily coming down and landing on the trees and cars and every possible surface available.

It was a beautiful winter's wonderland, but not one anyone wished to see in April.

Susan dressed quickly and warmly putting on snow pants. Instead of her morning run her exercise would be spent clearing snow off her car. Fortunately, the condo fees paid for snow clearance off the parking area, but the morning's snow had already dumped at least six inches of the white stuff and the car park was beginning to get snowed under again even though it had already been cleared once.

The team arrived in dribs and drabs, the adrenaline of the past few days having been drained out of them. They all looked tired, and Susan was relieved that their ordeal was now over and that everyone could finally be able to go back home.

"Good morning, everyone, on this cold and snowy morning. You will all be pleased to know that we will be wrapping up this investigation. We have conclusive results back from the DNA testing. It appears that traces of DNA from Pippa Hargreaves were found on Chris Saul's neck and on Sally Albright. The DNA swabs taken from the doctor did not match any of the other results. DNA from Pippa's hairbrush proves that she had not only murdered Matt Irons and James Kidd but had indeed actually also murdered Chris Saul and Sally Albright.

"On top of that, Pippa Hargreaves confessed that she had colluded with the doctor. He slipped the Flunitrazepam or Rohypnol, into both Chris and Sally's drinks. She then came back later that night and administered the lethal injection.

Constable Ryan interrupted Susan. "But ma'am, according to The Little Inn's registrar, Pippa Hargreaves checked out Saturday afternoon and presumably drove back to Toronto."

Susan smiled benignly at her Constable Ryan.

"Ah, Constable, never presume anything, but yes you're right, she did check out of the Inn on Saturday. However, according to Peggy Grierson, she stayed with Doctor Glover on Saturday and Sunday night as she didn't have to be back on duty at the hospital until Monday evening."

"Now the doctor insisted that he at least finish off the job by going after Lynda Forbes himself. When he did not succeed and then killed himself, Pippa decided that she would try to get at Lynda herself and she almost succeeded. Thanks to Tom Blair, the security at the hospital was increased, and that managed to thwart Pippa in her endeavours to murder the last person on the doctor's list."

Constable Ryan put her hand up again. Susan smiled to herself. She could afford to be kind and patient to this young woman as the case was now over. In many ways, she reminded Susan of herself thirty years ago when she was at the start of her own career. It was a tough call being a female officer in such a predominantly male profession and one had to be pushy to get noticed.

"Yes, Constable?"

"Ma'am, why did Pippa go back to Suzy Ball?"

"Good question, officer. You need to understand obsessive attachment disorder to begin to acknowledge Pippa Hargreaves's illness. She needed to latch herself on to someone and Suzy was still an old flame and lived just down the road from Bayfield. She had just lost the love of her life, Doctor Glover, and was devastated. You have to remember that it is an illness. She is currently being assessed by a group of psychologists."

There was an audible sigh and then a shuffle of feet as the team took in this information. Unfortunately, in so many cases where the accused was declared mentally insane, their sentences appeared far too lenient, and the police often felt frustrated with the verdict.

Susan continued, "However, there is some good news, everyone. Rose Blair regained consciousness and has woken up from her coma. The two drugged women, Lynda and Kate, have also made a good recovery and are absolutely fine. I have yet to write up my final report, but I do have to tell each and every one of you that you will all be recommended for commendations for your professional handling of this case. Thank you all for a job well done."

Constable Ryan felt her eyes well up with pride. This had been her first serious murder case and now there might possibly be a commendation to follow. She had to pinch herself to see that she was not dreaming.

FORTY-SIX

The doctor gave Rose a clean bill of health although he warned her that trauma to the head could sometimes take years to heal. He said that she might experience dizzy spells, headaches, or eye problems, and as such he recommended that she not drive for two months. That came as a bit of a shock to Rose, but she was still so thrilled to be alive that it seemed a small price to pay.

Susan came to visit carrying a huge bouquet and a large box of chocolates. She asked Rose what she could remember.

"Well, it's really strange," Rose said. "I remember everything up to going around to Lynda's house, but I have absolutely no recall of anything after. I don't know how I got my head injury and I certainly have no recollection of Kate and Lynda being drugged."

"Well, I'll tell you everything..." Susan spent the following half an hour relaying the whole sad story of the doctor and Pippa's obsession and the awful subsequent murders. By the time she had finished Rose's face had registered such concern that Susan regretted having revealed the case in all its gory, to her.

"So, please tell me that Peggy Grierson wasn't involved in all of this?" Rose asked.

"No, she said that the doctor had told her about DFI and how he had wanted to seek retribution, but she says that she never dreamt that he was serious. You know that she is heart broken over his death."

"Oh, poor Peggy," Rose said. "She will miss the doctor dearly. Oh my, it seems that I really missed out on all the action."

"Oh, but Rose, if you had not rushed in and attacked the doctor, he would have killed two innocent women. You're a hero. Kate and Lynda owe you their lives."

"Oh, well, put it that way I don't feel so bad. I still can't believe that Pippa Hargreaves, the romance writer, could have been such a psycho. She came over to our table at the Books and Brunch and seemed such a sweet, pretty young woman. Just goes to tell how looks can be misleading."

"Yes and looking at you I can tell that you need a good dose of rest right now. Tom, make sure that this wife of yours does rest. You know what she's like. Now I'm off to London to the Serious Crimes Division. I've got my final report to hand in and then Peter and I are flying to Aruba for a much-needed break. I'll see you both when I get back."

Susan kissed Rose and smiled at Tom. "Be good to her, Tom, she's very precious."

"I know," Tom said and gave Susan a big hug.

"Oh, by the way, there are two very excited women just waiting to come in to visit. Shall I send them in?"

"I know, I can hear my sister a mile off. Yes, send them in," Rose laughed.

Kate and Lynda entered carrying balloons and a large cake.

"What are you two up to?" Rose said, "It's not my birthday!"

"Oh, these are a Welcome Back to the Land of the Living celebration and we bought this as well." Lynda produced a large bottle of

Champagne, "We have to make a toast to the brave woman who saved our lives. Rose, we are beholden to you forever. Now, our other gift to you is that we are going to redecorate your kitchen while you rest. Kate is going to stay on to help look after you and we will both work on the kitchen together." Lynda winked at Tom. "Oh, and Tom is going to help too."

Rose clapped her hands together with delight and then Tom brought out his laptop and set it on the bedside table.

"You have a special phone call or should I say, FaceTime appointment with Anne, Allan, and Oliver, love." He clicked into FaceTime and sure enough there Anne and her little family were beaming out from the screen at Rose.

"Oh, Mom, you had us all so worried. Now, we've got some very special news to tell you. Dad already knows, but... we're having another baby."

A SNEAK PEEK AT MURDER AT THE RETREAT!

Tom pulled a long face as he flicked through the glossy leaflet in his hand.

"Are you really quite sure that you want to go on this couples retreat love?" He asked Rose who was preoccupied with packing an overnight bag.

"Oh Tom, of course I want to go. Besides, Anne sent it to us as a present, so we have to go. She'll no doubt want to know all about it and besides, I've never been on a couples retreat before. It could be quite good fun."

Tom shook his head. It all sounded so new age. "Freeing Your Inner Child," he read. "Be at One with Your Creativity, Embrace your Sexuality." He just knew that the book *Women are from Venus and Men from Mars* would also be part of the weekend's agenda. He let out a deep sigh. Well at least it was just for one weekend he thought as he picked up his pajamas and stuffed them into the bag.

Rose's friend, Lynda, recently back from West Palm Beach, had promised to take care of Ben and Puff, their beloved dogs, and she arrived just as Rose was putting their overnight bags into Tom's car.

"Perfect timing," Lynda said as she greeted Rose with a warm hug. Ben and Puff, hearing Lynda's voice, came charging out of the house, barking with excitement.

"Oh, you lovely puppies. We're going to have such fun together." Lynda turned to Rose and said, "Is it okay if they spend the weekend at our house? It would be much easier for me."

"Gosh, yes, of course as long as you don't mind all the dog hair!"

Rose had a mental image flash through her mind of Lynda and Barry's immaculate living room with Puff and Ben jumping up on their white sofa and leaving black hairs everywhere.

"Okay, then, let's go." Lynda said taking the dog leashes from Tom who held them out to her, "Have a great weekend away." Lynda waved goodbye and was then dragged off by two exuberant dogs who didn't give either Rose or Tom a second glance.

"Shallow creatures," Tom muttered as he got into his car and waited for Rose to join him.

Ivy Cottage Retreat was nestled down a small lane just past the Ben Miller Inn. The Maitland River meandered slowly alongside the road and shimmered and sparkled under the late May sun. Summer had finally arrived, and green leaves now covered the trees and daffodils nodded their golden heads in the light breeze.

As Rose and Tom pulled up in front of the not-so cottagey looking building, more like an old red brick farm house than anything else, a young woman dressed entirely in black came tripping down the front entrance and waved Tom over to park beneath a clump of maple trees by the side of the house. There were already a few other cars parked neatly side by side under the shade of the trees.

"Are you quite sure that you want to do this, love?" Tom asked as he manoeuvred around the cars already parked and deftly reversed his Audi TT in between a Range Rover and a Ford Escape.

"You really are reluctant to enter into the spirit of this weekend, aren't you? Look, it will be fine, just wait and see, try to keep an open mind."

Tom sighed and nodded his head. This trip was more about Rose and her recovery than anything else. Although, personally a weekend in Toronto would have suited him much better, but he knew that their daughter Anne had the best of intentions. After the trauma of the previous summer when Rose had almost died from a severe head injury, this getaway was supposed to be recuperative as much as anything else.

They entered the farm house building and noticed immediately the calm, Zen-like atmosphere. Tingly music played through unseen speakers. The young woman from the car-park smiled at them and said, "Welcome to Ivy Cottage. Here is the itinerary for this weekend's retreat. If you follow me, I'll show you to your room and you can freshen up before we have our welcome session. It's at 4:00 p.m."

Thank goodness we have our own bathroom, Rose thought as she glanced at the big claw footed bath and antiquated taps. Their room was at the end of the corridor and inside a four-poster bed fairly dominated the otherwise rather small room. The walls were papered with a rather chintzy flowery pattern and the furniture looked antique and far too heavy for Rose's liking. A tiny washroom with an equally small shower was squeezed into the corner of the room. The space however was light and airy and looked clean and fresh.

Rose bounced on the bed and then lay down. "Come on Tom, stop pulling a face. Just try to be positive. Let's look at the agenda. Um... welcome at 4:00, dinner at 6:00, followed by couple's trivia, and then a meditation before lights out at 10:00 p.m. That doesn't sound too bad, does it?"

Tom had taken his shoes off and was lying next to Rose on the bed contemplating the ceiling. He closed his eyes and tried to imagine that they were in a smart hotel in Toronto and not in the strange farmhouse called Ivy Cottage.

It somehow irked him that the house was called Ivy Cottage when it plainly was a rambling, old farmhouse with absolutely no sign of any ivy anywhere.

"So, Tom, what do you think?" Rose looked at her husband who seemingly had fallen asleep. Her question, however, was never answered as there was a loud knock on their bedroom door.

Rose leapt off the bed and opened it. Standing in her stockinged feet stood an exotically beautiful woman. She was a few inches taller than Rose, but whereas Rose was rather plump and round, this woman was slim and attractively turned out in a tight-fitting navy-blue sheath dress, set off by a huge oval opal pendant with matching earrings.

Her thick, chestnut brown hair cascaded in curls down to her shoulders and her creamy beige skin glowed with good health. Her lips were painted bright red, which on another woman might have looked cheap, but on her it served only to accentuate the fullness of her sensual lips. She was a beautiful woman and for a moment Rose felt a pang of jealousy envelope her.

"Can I help you?" Rose enquired wondering just who the apparition was and what she was doing knocking on their door.

"I was just wondering where the welcome was to take place? Oh, by the way," she said, holding out an elegantly manicured hand, "my name is Juliet. I do hope that I didn't wake you." Rose noticed her glancing over at a sleepy looking Tom now sitting up on the bed.

Rose took her hand which was surprisingly cool and soft.

"Oh, no, we weren't sleeping. My name is Rose, and this is my husband, Tom. You know, in answer to your question I'm not sure where the welcome session will be. I would imagine that it would be in the living room. We haven't checked out the facilities here yet. It's a bit strange being called a cottage though when it clearly is a farmhouse, isn't it?"

Juliet smiled and answered, "Ah ha, now that is something I can explain to you. If you look outside your bedroom window, you'll see a little foot path. It leads to the sweetest log cabin which is all covered in ivy. Presumably that's the original Ivy Cottage."

"Gosh, how did you discover that?"

"Oh, Harry and I arrived here hours ago and explored the

grounds and the house. It's all been a bit weird as nobody seemed to be around until a young woman dressed in black appeared and showed us to our room. I've been waiting for someone else to arrive for ages as I was beginning to feel somewhat apprehensive with just the two of us in this creepy, old building."

As Juliet was talking, Rose overheard footsteps in the hall as another couple was shown to their room. Rose looked at her watch. It was only 2:45 p.m., they still had over an hour to go before their welcome session.

I could kill for a cup of tea, she thought, as Juliet left to go back to her room and Rose closed the door.

"Tom, do you mind if I go and explore? I'll see if I can find a place to get us both a nice cup of tea. I won't be long." She bent over and gave Tom a quick kiss on his cheek and left the room quietly.

Walking back down the hallway, Rose overheard voices coming from several of the neighbouring bedrooms. The other couples' retreat guests were finally arriving.

Downstairs however, was still very quiet apart from the tingly sound of music. Rose walked to the back of the house rationalizing that kitchens generally were found not in the front of old homes but normally hidden away at the back. Sure enough, a small, galley-like kitchen was annexed to the side of a very large dining room.

Rose stepped in and immediately spied a kettle. *Now for the tea and cups,* she thought, opening and closing cupboards in her quest for a cup of tea. She had just spotted a box of tea bags when the sound of raised voices caught her attention and Rose immediately recognized Juliet's husky voice.

"Stop being so possessive Harry. I told you that I only met him for one drink. You know that James and I go back years. He's one of my oldest friends from university, plus the fact that he's happily married. Can't I have my own friends, now?"

Rose held her breath as she listened to the angry response, presumably from Harry, Juliet's husband.

"I just don't trust you, Julie. After your past behaviour, do you truly blame me? Look, if you want a divorce I'll give you one. I can't take the lies and deceit anymore, that's all."

"Oh, Harry, why do you think that I booked this couples retreat for us. I love you. I only wish you could understand that!"

Rose didn't hear any more of the conversation as suddenly the young woman who had greeted them popped her head around the door and said in a rather steely voice, "Can I help you?"

Rose almost jumped out of her skin, "Oh... yes, well, I really would love a cup of tea."

"Refreshments are in the living room," the woman said, clearly peeved to find Rose poking around the kitchen. "It's this way," and she pointed back to the front of the house. Rose followed her directions, turning as she left the hall to try to see where Juliet and her husband had been having their heated discussion.

The living room was at the front of the house and it was quite delightful. A large room with a stone fireplace opened out onto a beautiful sun lounge. There were colourful scatter cushions and bean bags on the carpeted floor as well as several comfortable arm chairs.

In the corner of the room a table had been set up with flasks of coffee, tea, and juice, along with plates of banana loaf and butter tarts with side plates and colourful serviettes. Newspapers and magazines were fanned out on a coffee table.

It all looked well organized. It would be much nicer having tea in the living room rather than up in their bedroom, thought Rose as she turned to go and get Tom.

ABOUT THE AUTHOR

Over the past thirty years Judy has written twenty novellas, various collections of poetry and a number of plays. Judy wrote her first full length novel in 2013 and developed it into a series called the Rose Blair Murder Mysteries all set in the sleepy village of Bayfield on the beautiful shores of Lake Huron in Ontario, Canada.

Judy and her husband reside in Bayfield with their beloved dog Susie and cat Thomas and enjoy visits from their children and grand-children.

After retiring Judy and her husband took on a new challenge in their lives. Purchasing land on the outskirts of Bayfield they have planted a six acre vineyard and are in the process of designing and building a boutique winery.

Life is beautiful and sweet. I feel so very blessed with all my wonderful family and friends who continually surround me with their love.